Death Before Compline

Short Stories
by Sharan Newman

Death Before Compline

Short Stories
by Sharan Newman

Baqwyn
Books

Tempe, Arizona
2012

Published by Bagwyn Books, an imprint of the Arizona Center for Medieval and Renaissance Studies (ACMRS), Tempe, Arizona.

Table of Contents

Introduction

The seven stories in this collection were written between 1996 and 2011. They have been re-edited especially for this edition, mainly because I can't resist the chance to improve on my own work. All of them are about the characters in my mystery series, set in France and other parts of Europe in the mid-twelfth century.

For those unfamiliar with the series, here is an overview.

Catherine Levendeur is a bright girl living in Paris in the 1130s. The daughter of a merchant, Hubert, who married a member of the minor nobility, Madeleine, she has an older brother, Guillaume, and a younger sister, Agnes. Guillaume has taken advantage of his mother's connections, married well, and become a castellan north of Paris. While in the first book, *Death Comes as Epiphany*, he fades from the others, so much so that I forgot all about him for quite a while.

As the first book opens, Catherine is a student at the Paraclete, the convent founded by Peter Abelard for his lover/wife, Heloise. Not having taken her vows yet, she is sent home by Heloise to investigate a manuscript that may have been altered to make the convent appear to be a hotbed of heresy. Catherine finds much more, including an unusual hermit, a lascivious uncle, and a pale blond scholar from England, Edgar.

By the end of the book, Catherine has discovered family secrets, caught a murderer, and decided that perhaps she wasn't meant to be a nun after all.

The Devil's Door also begins at the Paraclete, but Catherine is only there until Edgar returns from England for their wedding. One evening a badly beaten woman is brought in. The nuns try to save her, but cannot. Catherine and Edgar spend their honeymoon uncovering who murdered her and why. This story, as all in the series, began with a puzzle from history. There was a debate between the monks of Vauluisant and the nuns of the Paraclete over some land that each claimed. The settlement they reached seemed odd to me. While murder was probably not involved, I solved the puzzle to my own satisfaction.

The third book *The Wandering Arm*, takes Catherine and Edgar back to Paris. The trade in relics of the saints was big business in medieval Europe. Everything from cloaks to body parts were sold as being associated with saints. People even claimed to have the baby teeth and foreskin of Jesus, these being the only parts he would have left behind at the Ascension. However, people were not so credulous as to believe without investigation. It was important to know where the relic came from and trace the history of it. In this case, I discovered that a priest, who had wanted to become bishop of Salisbury, had made off with some relics when he was not given the job. It was thought that one of the relics was the arm of the Anglo-Saxon saint Aldhelm. Doing detective work of my own, I decided that it wasn't. However, that was after I had finished writing the book.

This book is about more than relics, though. One of my ongoing themes is the day-to-day interaction of Jews and Christians at this time. Catherine once again has a body literally fall on her, that of a Jewish merchant. His connection to Christian relic traders shows the amount of contact and business dealings between the two communities. I was amazed at the number of charters and other records that show agreements between Christians and Jews, even to joint ownership of property. In each book there is an undercurrent of the tension between having dealings with neighbors who happen to be of another faith and the official stand that Jews were stubborn in their refusal to admit Jesus was the Messiah and must be converted.

The fourth mystery, *Strong as Death*, was written because I had always wanted to go on the pilgrimage to Santiago de Compostella. For over a thousand years, pilgrims have made this journey to northern Spain. A friend and I went for the two weeks before Easter. It was an amazing experience. There were people from all over the world, some going as an act of religious devotion or penance, some just for the adventure. Catherine and Edgar make the trip because Catherine has had several miscarriages and stillbirths, a common problem almost up to the present. In desperation, they decide to ask the saint for a healthy child. Of course other people are making the pilgrimage for less honorable reasons, and soon the bodies start to pile up. Catherine's father, Hubert, and her cousin, Solomon, come with them and both find their lives changed by encounters with two very different women.

Cursed in the Blood was not a book I'd intended to write. It all began in a pub in Oxford. I was researching *The Wandering Arm* and heard that David Rollason, a professor at Durham, had done his dissertation on the theft of relics. But David was no longer interested in the topic. He had been doing work on the Prince-Bishops of Durham, in the north of England. In the twelfth century there were at least two who were not exactly holy. He thought they would make a good book. I said I'd write it if he could get me into the Cathedral archives. The next year I spent a month happily sitting in the old monks' refectory going through manuscripts and books.

One day I went down into what had been the cloister. As I came out of the library, I saw two Templars and a knight in armor stroll by. One of the Templars was smoking. For a moment I thought I'd stepped into a parallel universe. Then I saw the cameras. They were making a film of *Ivanhoe.*

Cursed in the Blood was my chance to explore the life of the average citizen caught up in a civil war. In the case of Durham, there was a war within a war. Catherine and Edgar are separated and she and their new baby must find him in a land where she only speaks the language of the conquerors. I also discovered more about Edgar's not-so-loving family, particularly his father. And, as I was writing the scene where Edgar returns to his home near the Scottish border, I suddenly discovered that he had a half-sister, Margaret, who was nine years old. I don't recall planning to invent her; she just appeared and became an important part of the rest of the series.

For *The Difficult Saint* I took the whole family off to Trier on the Moselle River, mainly because I had an invitation to do research at the Institute for the Study of Jewish History at the University there and I'd always wanted to visit. The town was Roman, then one of the cities of Constantine the Great, the first Christian emperor. There are buildings still there from those times, overlaid with medieval and finally modern buildings. They also make a very good sparkling wine.

But wine with bubbles hadn't been invented in the twelfth century, so the reason Catherine and Edgar go there is because Catherine's sister, Agnes, is marrying a local lord. Sadly, she is soon widowed and there is a suspicion that she may have killed her new husband through poisoning or witchcraft. Even though they don't get along that well, Catherine is not about to let her sister be condemned.

By this time, the Second Crusade is being planned. King Louis VII of France and his queen, Eleanor of Aquitaine, are going. As happened in the First Crusade, the first victims are the Jews of the Rhineland. There is another murder, tragically not fiction, of a Jewish man near Trier. Bernard, abbot of Clairvaux, who had preached the crusade, rushes to Trier to try to stop the killing. The title of *The Difficult Saint* was stolen from my friend Brian Patrick McGuire's biography of Bernard. But he is not the saint in the book. This was a time of upheaval. Not only was Europe being roused to protect the Holy Land, a new heresy was making its way in from the Balkans. Catherine and her family are caught in the middle of politics, religion, war, and family, all of which upset their lives.

I hadn't intended to write *To Wear the White Cloak*. I thought one book about the crusade was enough. Then I realized how much France was affected by the departure of the king, along with many fighting men and most of the treasury. One group that got stuck with the mundane preparations was the Templars. Louis had left a regent, to whom he wrote home for money like a college freshman. But the Templars, then a new and popular order, were the ones who arranged to ship provisions and men east.

I found the plot in three charters. One was from the city of Paris and concerned the gift to the Templars of some land and an oven. The charter had so many clauses that it was clear it would be years before the Templars saw anything from it. I think the woman was a social climber and just wanted to say she had donated, even though they couldn't collect until after she died. The second charter was from a Templar collection. This stated that, if a wealthy miller in the south of France became a Templar, his son could marry the local lord's daughter. Clearly, class distinctions weren't as rigid as many think. Finally, another charter from Paris stated that there were one hundred thirty Templars present to witness another gift. All I once I thought, "What if there should have been one hundred thirty-one?"

Everything evolved from that. Isn't it easy when someone explains it?

By now the reader should be getting the idea that I love medieval France, even if they didn't have champagne yet. For one thing, even though I've been studying the period for going on forty years (a terrifying thought) I can still be surprised by a new discovery. Sometimes it simply involves looking at an event in a new way.

That is what happened with *Heresy*, I wanted to set a book at the 1148 Council of Reims. I was explaining to my editor about what a cool gathering it was, how the pope was there and there were all these decisions ranging from a divorce to a clearly insane prophet. When I finished, there was a long silence from the phone. Finally she asked, "You do plan on killing somebody, don't you?" Never fear. Catherine goes to Reims to help her friend Astrolabe defend himself from a charge of heresy. Along the way she's attacked, insulted, and goes undercover as a beggar. She also finds she has to rethink her beliefs about just what heresy really is.

After eight bouts with murder, mayhem, and motherhood, I decided to give Catherine a break. Therefore *The Outcast Dove* is Solomon's book and my personal favorite. Solomon is a not very observant Jew with an eye for the ladies. He has no intention of converting and is highly cynical about the devoutness of most of the people around him. On the other hand, he is fascinated by mysticism. He believes that there is a reason for all the madness around him and, if he only had the key, he could make sense of what, to him, is a chaotic world.

I fell in love with him early on in the series. Unfortunately, he has fallen in love with Edgar's young sister, Margaret. I didn't tell him to do this. There are so many reasons why the whole thing is impossible, but neither one of them will listen to me. They seem to expect me to figure out a way for them to be happy. It's a dreadful responsibility and I have only a glimmer of how it might be done.

The Outcast Dove takes place in Toulouse, France, and northern Spain. Solomon is traveling with a party of Jewish traders when one of them is murdered. In this I explore the lives of Jews in Southern France, where they were much more assimilated than in the north. But as perpetual aliens in a Christian society, there is always the possibility that everything could change in a moment. Some, like Solomon, spent most of their time in the secular world, but many Jews were fervently observant. One reason for this is that it is easy to slide away from faith when almost everyone else is against one's beliefs. It's necessary to have a firm set of rules that set one apart from others.

In *The Outcast Dove*, Solomon learns to respect the strength that has kept his religion intact for so many millennia. He also sees how blind adherence to a strict interpretation of the law can cause tragedy.

After doing extensive research in Toulouse and spending a year with Solomon's angst, I decided to just have fun. *The Witch in the Well* is half a fantasy and half a country manor mystery. Catherine, Edgar, and their children are summoned to the castle of her apparently immortal grandfather. There they find Agnes, with her family and Madeleine, their mother. Madeleine has been at the convent of Tart for years, cared for by the nuns after she decided Catherine was a saint. She is still only loosely attached to the real world. A family member is found dead, Madeleine standing over him with a bloody knife. What follows includes a chase through underground passages, old family hatreds, possible attack, and a touch of magic.

So, that's the series so far. These stories were all written on request but each one focuses on an aspect of the family and of medieval France that I was happy to explore.

I hope you enjoy them.

The Beast Without

The stories in this collection are arranged by the course of Catherine's life, so this first story is actually the most recently published. It appeared in Tales of the Shadowmen *in January of 2011. The premise of this annual anthology is that each story must contain a character from French literature. The stories have included famous French authors, such as Jules Verne, and also characters from English literature, like Lord Peter Wimsey. For my contribution, I chose a story of Marie de France, who wrote in the late twelfth century. We aren't certain who she was, but many of her tales, like this one, are based in Breton legends. In this case, a young Catherine enters into a world where the monsters of the forest are real.*

Broceliande, Brittany, 1134

From the safety of the forest he watched the lady ride by.

He thought she would be wan with grief but she was laughing with one of her friends, the two of them balancing sparrow hawks on their wrists. Servants and beaters ran alongside. He moved back into the shadows. They couldn't find him, not like this.

The bells on the jesses of the birds jingled in his ears as he slunk away through the underbrush. He would have to travel far to find his dinner tonight. His body ached with love, longing, anger and, overpowering them all, hunger.

Paris, the same day

Catherine shimmied over the side wall, scraping her palms as she fell into the garden. Her heart was still pounding in terror. She hurried to the water to try to clean herself off before her mother...

"Catherine!"

Too late. Catherine turned. Seeing the look on her mother's face, she said nothing, but followed her into the house.

The home was comfortable, showing the prosperity of its owner, the merchant Hubert Levendeur. It rose three stories on a side street near the *Grève* with a spacious kitchen and chicken run in the back. The walls enclosed a lawn speckled with fruit trees that sloped down to a stream. Inside the house was decorated with fine wall hangings, more chairs than family members and soft cushions of velvet. The tall girl with black braids in a tangle and a torn robe spattered with mud and blood was decidedly out of place.

Her mother certainly thought so.

"What am I to do with you, Catherine?" Madeleine demanded. "You're fourteen, not a child any more. Many girls your age are already married. Look at yourself."

Catherine stared at the floor, noticing that her bare toes were also tracking mud across the rushes. Her shoes had come off when she climbed the stone wall. She had no answer. Any explanation would only increase her mother's wrath.

There was a step behind her. Madeleine turned her anger on the new arrival without pausing for breath.

"This is all you're fault, Hubert!" She glared at her husband. "You let her learn Latin. You laugh at her antics. You encourage her to ignore her sewing and you let her dress like a peasant. She doesn't even have shoes on!"

Catherine tried to curl her toes under her skirts.

"She's not fit for marriage," Madeleine continued. "No one could provide a dowry large enough. She wouldn't last a month in a convent with all her questions. What will become of her?"

Her voice dwindled from outrage to despair.

Hubert paid no attention. He grabbed his daughter in a tight embrace. Catherine gasped at the force of it. Were there tears in his eyes?

"Papa?" She realized that he knew. "*Saint Agatha, save me from his anger!*" she prayed.

"Are you all right?" His voice was breathless. "Did they hurt you? What did they do? Tell me at once!"

Madeleine stared at them both; it dawned on her that Catherine had done more than fall in the mud in the garden.

"They were students, Papa." She couldn't look in his eyes. "I took the short cut between the church and the Bishop's palace. They pushed me against a wall and tried to . . ." She couldn't say it. "I screamed and someone heard and chased them away."

"Oh, my dear Lord!" Madeleine reached out and felt her daughter: face, arms, side, back and front, searching for signs of damage.

Hubert's panic was fading now that he knew she was safe. "Pagan, the milk peddler, heard her. He clanked the cans and shouted at them. Since this one ran, too, he thought she might have been there willingly."

"Never! I wouldn't!" Catherine swore. "I think they followed me from the lecture."

Hubert ignored her. "He came and found me immediately and I raced here, not knowing what I would find. How could you do this?" He glared at Catherine.

"That's what comes of Latin," Madeleine said with a kind of triumph. "Now her reputation is ruined. No one will marry her."

Both parents considered the state of their elder daughter. Catherine considered it herself. What was she to do? Marriage didn't seem appealing, from what she'd seen of it. A convent was probably her fate if they would let her copy books instead of sewing. She enjoyed helping her father keep the records of his trade, but didn't know what good that would be to nuns. As for curbing her tongue, she suspected that only frequent beatings would teach her that, something even her mother was too soft-hearted to administer.

She looked so apologetic and frightened that Madeleine relented and hugged her, carefully, around the dirt.

"Go clean yourself," she said quietly. "Are you sure they did nothing more than grab you?"

Catherine nodded. "I'm sorry. I just wanted to hear the talk on universals. I didn't think anyone would want to hurt me."

"No, you didn't think." Hubert shook his head. "This can't go on. It's time we found a convent for you, at least to let you be educated in safety. Now go. Obey your mother for once."

For once, Catherine did as she was told and left the room.

That night, as she lay curled up in bed against the warm body of her little sister, Agnes, Catherine could hear the sound of her parents' voices from the alcove on the floor below. She couldn't make out the words, but the worried tone suggested that she was the topic.

At one time, her mother's voice rose, "Not Fontevraud, it's full of whores and men."

Catherine sighed. Her future did not look promising.

Two weeks later Catherine found herself on a barge sailing down the Loire River, another parcel in her father's stock of goods to trade, along with the barrels of Cistercian wine, incense, and spices. To her parents' astonishment, she had given only token resistance to the news that they were sending her to stay with the nuns at the abbey of St. Georges in Rennes in the wilds of Brittany.

The men who had followed her into the alleyway had frightened her to the core. Paris was her home. Yes, there were dangers. She could fall into the river or be run over by some nobleman on a horse. The king's son had been thrown from his horse and killed when a loose pig had crossed his path in the Paris streets. Fires were common. But she had never before been afraid of people. She was not so naïve that she didn't understand what the men had intended to do to her. But no one had ever so much as leered at her, as far as she knew. What had changed?

She began to wonder if her mother's constant warnings might actually be worth heeding.

Catherine watched a village glide by. It was a collection of a few houses with a clearing reaching to a wooden docking place. Children were gathering sticks for the fire. Two men were sawing a log. It would be winter soon.

When they arrived at Nantes, Hubert and Catherine were given a room near the palace of Bishop Brice. The wine was rolled into the cellar to enhance the bishop's table for the coming year. Hubert requested an audience with Brice for the following day. He not only wanted to show him some fine amber from Muscovy but he also needed documents to allow him safe passage north to Rennes.

"We'll be hiring horses here," he told his daughter. "You can ride pillion behind me. It won't be comfortable but it's only a couple of days. I want you to stay close to me at *all* times. Do you understand?"

Catherine nodded.

"This isn't a stroll to St. Denis, child." He had to impress her with the danger. "There are bandits and wild animals and demons lurking everywhere. The other traders and I are bringing armed guards, but they can't protect you if you wander off."

"Yes, Papa, I promise." Catherine's eyes were round with sincerity.

Hubert had his doubts. He wondered if he could chain her to his belt, but couldn't quite bring himself to humiliate her that much. He hoped he wouldn't regret it.

The road north was little more than a track. Branches hung low over it. They slapped at the riders, dropping dry leaves into their hair and down their tunics. Catherine amused herself by catching at the leaves as she rode by. Her continual movement was driving her father to distraction.

"Can't you stay still, girl?" he complained.

She leaned against his and whispered in his ear. "I have to go to the bathroom, Papa."

Hubert sighed. "We'll stop at the next clearing. It shouldn't be long."

Catherine groaned. It seemed like hours before the path widened to a clearing with a spring to water horses and men. She slid off the horse and hurried into the wood.

"Don't go far!" Hubert shouted behind her.

Catherine was certain that she couldn't go more than the few steps required for privacy. She selected a spot where she could squat in the undergrowth next to an oak tree. After checking to see which way the ground sloped, she hoisted her skirts, leaning against the tree trunk. She gave a long sigh of relief.

She was just about to stand when she heard a deep growl nearby. Catherine peered cautiously around the brush and her breath stopped.

Not ten paces from her there stood an enormous black wolf. It was staring directly at her, teeth bared. She tried not to move a muscle as it slowly approached. She wanted to scream but was too terrified.

The wolf gained speed as it came closer. Its jaws opened wide and it leapt.

"Mother Mary, save my soul," Catherine whispered. She shut her eyes tightly, steeling herself for the horrible attack.

She felt the air move as he flew past her, smelled the musk of his fur. From the other side of the tree there was a scream abruptly cut off. The wolf's growl became a howl of fury. A moment later he appeared, no more than a hand's-breadth from her face. The fur around his mouth was dripping with blood. His golden eyes stared into her blue ones and, in that moment, fear left her.

The wolf lowered his head and vanished into the dark woods.

Catherine exhaled and tried to stand. Her limbs were shaking and she could do no more than hold on to the oak as she tried to calm her racing heart. What had happened? The expression in the wolf's eyes had been almost intelligent, overflowing with sadness. But there was blood on his muzzle.

"Catherine!" Hubert's voice rang with panic.

"Here, Papa, here!" she called back. A moment later she was wrapped in his strong arms.

"*Siwazh din!*" One of the Breton guards had followed them. "Look at this!"

Hubert turned to look and immediately tried to cover her eyes with his hand. Catherine squirmed away. There in the brush behind the tree lay the body of a man with his throat torn out. His blood ran down the dry leaves and pooled on the ground. His short tunic was of rough wool, his pantaloons made of animal skins sewn together. Next to him on the ground was a long knife.

It took a moment for Catherine to make sense of this.

"He saved my life," she said in wonder.

"The poor man!" Hubert shook his head. "He drew the wolf's attention from you. But he wasn't quick enough with the knife. I wish I knew his name. We shall have Masses said for his soul."

Catherine shook her head, too, very slowly. "Papa, I didn't mean him. I think he was hiding in wait to rob me. It was the wolf who saved me."

Hubert patted her back. "Now, now, pet. You've had a terrible shock. Let's get you back. We need to reach the town of Fougerai before dark. I won't risk a night in the open after this. Here, you! Viard!" He gestured toward the guard. "Throw the body on one of the pack mules. We need to give him a decent burial."

Viard and his friend, Guémaroc, lifted the man's body and tied him to the mule. All the time they muttered to each other in tones of disapproval. Hubert heard them but was concerned more with Catherine than disgruntled guards.

Catherine said nothing as the party moved on, more rapidly now. She was still shaking. It didn't make sense. Why should a wolf rescue her from a brigand of the forest? And what was the word the guards kept repeating, *bleiz-laveret*? A shiver ran through her as she remembered tales a neighbor used to tell of her childhood in Brittany, of monsters and sprites that lived in the forests and caves. According to her, one could never trust that the world one went to sleep in would be the same one woke to.

Was the man really a man, Catherine pondered. And was the wolf really a wolf? If only she could have looked in the man's eyes.

The wolf loped far into the forest before he stopped at a stream to wash out his mouth. His stomach roiled at the taste of human flesh. And yet, deep inside, he knew he could get used to it, even crave it. He drank long, trying to wash away even the memory of the taste. If that happened, nothing could save him.

The party rode in silence and haste to the town. The guards went first to the home of the mayor to deliver the body. After asking several people who apparently spoke only Breton, Hubert finally was able to find a room for himself and his daughter. The other merchants made do at a tavern, where they regaled the local men with the story of the strange wolf, even though none of them had actually seen it.

Viard returned with the mayor and his wife, Furnez. The men retired to the tavern while Furnez saw to Catherine.

"You poor child!" she exclaimed. "What madness possessed your father to bring you on such a trip?"

"I'm to stay with the nuns at Saint Georges, "Catherine explained. "To learn how to behave properly and not get into trouble."

Furnez laughed. "Well, that may not be the best place to do it, *moumoun.* The abbess is well above eighty years old and I've heard that the discipline is not the best. But time enough to face that. For now, let's get you washed and into clean robes."

She took Catherine's hand. "You're freezing, little one! Viard said you'd had a near escape from the Wolf. Hot spiced wine for you, too."

Catherine let herself be led to the mayor's house to be fed and spoiled and to play with Furnez's two small children until water had been heated for a wooden tub in the kitchen. As she scrubbed herself, Catherine listened to Furnez helping the children recite their evening prayers. They said the *Nostre Pere* and an *Ave Maria*. Then they added a prayer to a saint Catherine didn't know. "Lady Ségénex, protect us this night from the korrigans and their children, the poulpiquets, from goblins and spirits and the Black Knight of the woods, amen."

When the nurse had taken them to their bed and Catherine was dry and dressed, she asked Furnez about the prayer.

"Don't you ask for protection from the evil things that fly by night?" the woman asked her.

"Yes, but mostly demons and the spirits that suck out children's souls," Catherine said. "And who is saint Ségénex?"

Furnez smiled. "The lady is the ancient guardian of our people. She was once a pagan priestess and a great magician but was converted by Joseph of Arimathea. When she died, she refused to go to heaven as long as her people needed her. There are so many powerful creatures that still roam this land. The poor saint may be with us until the End Times."

Catherine could well believe this. Even Nantes had a feel of being only at the edge of the Christian world. She decided to tell Furnez about her strange encounter with the wolf.

"He looked straight at me and he seemed sorry for me," she tried to explain. "Papa says I have too much imagination. But I still don't know why he didn't attack me."

Furnez had already heard the story from Viard and Guémaroc. "Was the wolf black all over with a thick shiny coat and bright yellow eyes?"

Catherine nodded. "Gold. His eyes were golden as the moon when it first rises."

"I thought so." Furnez refilled her wine cup, adding only a little water. "Then it's a blessing that no one tried to kill it. That is Duke Conan's tame wolf."

"Then why didn't it have a collar or a muzzle?" Catherine asked. She wasn't surprised that the duke had a pet wolf. The nobility had all sorts of peculiar habits.

"I don't know that whole story," Furnez shrugged. "But I do know that it's a particular favorite of the duke and that it is supposed to be a model of *courtoisie*. If it killed a man, you can be certain it was to protect you from him."

Catherine was so sleepy from the wine that she had to be carried back to her room. The next morning she told Hubert what Furnez had said about the wolf.

"Papa, I believe that the wolf was once a man," she said earnestly.

Hubert rolled his eyes. "Catherine, have you been reading Ovid again?"

"No, Papa! You told the Archdeacon that he wasn't to loan me any more pagan authors." She made a face. The hurt from that still festered.

"If, as they say, the wolf belongs to the duke, then perhaps he was trained to protect," Hubert explained. "That's probably what the mayor's wife meant. But no one can truly tame a beast like that. Last night, one of the men at the tavern told me that recently at the duke's court the wolf took a dislike to one of the barons and tried to attack him. You see? The wild animal always breaks loose."

"I suppose." Catherine didn't believe him. "But perhaps the baron was a bad man. Perhaps the wolf can smell evil."

"Catherine," Hubert warned. "Why don't you save your argument for the nuns? I'm sure they know the situation better than either of us."

The next afternoon the party passed by the hunting lodge where Duke Conan was staying. The men all agreed that they should pay their respects to him. Each mentally went through their goods searching for something that Conan would discover he was in desperate need of.

They were told that the duke would see them as soon as he could. He sent out beer and sausage to help them pass the time.

"That's a proper lord," one of the merchants said as he took a long draft. "He remembers his duty to those . . ."

He stopped, the cup slipping from his fingers. He pointed at the shape coming out of the lodge.

"Wolf." He grabbed at the cup and emptied it down his throat without moving any other part of his body.

Catherine was still, this time in fascination rather than terror. The wolf seemed much more doglike here. It sniffed a passing cart and rubbed its side against a rough stone wall. No one patted it as they went by, but it seemed to be more from respect than nervousness. But there was no sign in him of human sensibility. Perhaps her father was right.

At that moment a short procession approached the lodge. There were two guards, a mule laden with packages and a woman, heavily veiled.

One of the men entered the lodge to announce the visitor. As she waited, the woman pushed her veil aside in order to see better.

Suddenly, the wolf froze, hackles stiff. It growled in much the same tone Catherine had heard in the forest. Before anyone could stop him, the wolf sprang at the woman, trapping her face in his fierce jaws.

"My God!" Hubert cried, but he could barely be heard over the pandemonium. Men with swords converged on the wolf as it dropped to the ground.

The woman was shrieking, trying to soak up the blood pouring down her face. Her veil and the front of her robe were stained vermilion. "Kill him!" she screamed. "Kill him!"

Her other guard raised his sword. The wolf paid no attention. His eyes never left the woman's face. With a gagging noise, he spat something on the ground.

It was her nose.

Hubert couldn't resist. "You see, Catherine? If you take in something savage, eventually it will turn on you."

"Yes, Papa," Catherine said absently. Then she ran toward the crowd. "Don't hurt him!" she cried. "Please don't hurt him!"

Oddly, others felt the same. The guard had been restrained. Servants lifted the lady down and wrapped her face in cloths. Someone carried her into the lodge. Shortly after that, the duke came out.

"What is this?" he demanded, looking at his pet. "This is the second time you have attacked my guests. I thought you were an enchanted wolf, a courtly animal. You have never even chased one of my deer." He turned to his men. "There's nothing for it; he'll have to be put down at once."

"No!" Catherine tried to throw herself between the beast and the blade. "He saved my life. I know he's not evil."

The duke was startled by her interruption. "Who are you?" he snapped. "No, never mind. Jago, kill him."

Catherine began to protest again, but it wasn't necessary. The servant sheathed his sword.

"Please, my lord," he said. "I think we should consider this a moment. This wolf has been at the court over a year and has been nothing but well-behaved. His courtesy has been the wonder of us all. Why would he suddenly attack two people?"

"This lady," another man spoke up. "She's Lantilde, the wife of Brochan, who was the first victim of the wolf. Perhaps the two of them have injured the animal somehow."

Conan regarded the wolf, who gazed up at him with the calm air of a knight prepared for death. The duke paused. He had grown very fond of his pet.

"Very well," he decided. "Put the animal in a cage. When the lady is able, I shall question her. Although how she could have offended a wolf is more than I can guess."

They went inside. Catherine started to follow but Hubert caught her.

"What are you thinking of? We don't belong to the court."

"I have to know what will happen to the wolf," Catherine explained. "I know he's more than a dumb animal, whatever you say. Even Duke Conan seems to think so."

Hubert sighed. "Don't worry, none of the others here intend to leave until the matter is resolved. This is a story we can use for years to gain entrance to the courts of other nobles. But you are not to simply wander into the lodge and make yourself at home. Your mother would be horrified."

The merchants set up their tents outside the lodge. If a few trades were made that evening, it was a bonus, but even if they lost money, not one of them would regret staying.

By the next morning, Lantilde's nose had stopped bleeding, although no one could replace it. She was carried into the courtyard on a litter and placed near the cage of the wolf. It growled at her a moment and then began to whimper, as if crying.

"I beg you, my lord," she cried, her voice muffled by the bandages. "Move me away from that monster."

The servant, Jago, had appointed himself advocate for the wolf.

"My lady," he began. "I grieve for your pain and disfiguration. You are the widow of Lord Paynel, my friend and one of the duke's most faithful knights, who vanished some time ago."

"Yes. His body was never found. We think he was killed by mad heretics."

The wolf stood alert, taking in every word. Catherine had managed to wiggle her way through to a spot near the cage. At the mention of the name Paynel, the wolf began to wag his tail. Catherine nodded in satisfaction. She knew she was right. Both Ovid and the Breton stories couldn't be mistaken.

Jago had also noted the response. He looked from the woman to the wolf and back again.

"My lord." He turned to the duke. "This animal has always shown itself to be gentle and docile, totally against the nature of a beast. I believe that there is a reason he hates this woman and her husband so. Since he cannot tell us, I suggest that she be put to the torture until she says what she did to the wolf."

Lantilde screamed. "Have I not been tortured enough by this unnatural creature? Look at me!"

Conan did. "It seems strange to me, Lady, that he only bit off your nose, rather than tearing out your throat. There are many mysteries in this land. My wolf may be one of them. Yes," he nodded to Jago. "Have her tortured."

"No! No!" Lantilde tried to sit up. "No, I'll tell you. Then you may understand how I have been tricked and humiliated. That monster is Paynel! He married me knowing that he was a man only half the week. I loved him to the point of folly. But when I learned what he really was, surely the spawn of a demon, I couldn't live with him any more."

Catherine gasped. It was one thing to have one's speculations proven true in theory. It was quite another to look at a wolf and wonder who was inside him.

"I might have denounced him to the bishop," Lantilde continued. "I could have had him slaughtered by hunters or burnt at the stake. Instead, all I did was to hide his clothes so he couldn't change back to human form. I made him live all his life as the fiend he had always been."

She lay back again, exhausted.

The duke considered her story. "Is this true?" he asked the wolf. It nodded vigorously.

There was silence as everyone tried to take in this revelation. Catherine thought of the clerics who had wanted to rape her in Paris. She wondered if at night they returned to their true forms or if they always managed to hide their demons inside. It would be easier if she could have seen their real shapes.

"There is one way to prove this," Jago told the duke. "Bring Paynel his clothes."

Lantilde seemed even more upset about that than about losing her nose, but she was finally convinced to send a servant back to her castle with instructions as to the hiding place of her husband's clothing.

While they waited, Catherine and her father sat on a bench and shared some bread and cheese. They didn't speak, but Hubert put her arm around her shoulders and hugged her. That was enough.

The servant arrived late that afternoon with a parcel that contained a rough tunic, a soft linen shirt and leather pants. In a bag, he carried Paynel's hose and boots.

The clothes were put into the cage with the wolf. Everyone waited.

Nothing happened.

The wolf sniffed at the clothes, looked at the crowd of expectant faces and huddled in one corner of the cage, his tail wrapped over his head.

Duke Conan was bewildered. "Perhaps the woman is insane," he suggested. "She may have killed her husband and made up the story in case his clothes were found."

Catherine had been watching the wolf closely. She stepped forward.

"My lord?" She bowed as low as she could without overbalancing.

He looked at her. "Who . . . ? Oh, yes, the little girl who says my wolf saved her. What do you want?"

"Um, well." Catherine knew she was going to sound foolish, but that had never stopped her before. "I think he doesn't want to get dressed in front of everyone. He may change back naked."

Someone snickered. Conan gave the offender a sharp look.

"Paynel always was a private person," he said. "Never liked to bathe with others. Very well. Jago, take the wolf and the clothing to my bedroom. Leave him there and we'll see."

Jago opened the cage and picked up the clothing. The wolf followed him with alacrity. Jago returned a few moments later.

People milled about, not sure what to do next. But they didn't have to worry. Almost at once there was the clop of boots on the wooden steps. A man appeared, his dark beard long and tangled, his hair matted with grease. But those who had known Paynel recognized him at once. He was embraced by his friends before he came to kneel before the duke.

"My Lord," his voice cracked. "Forgive me from hiding my affliction from you. It has been a deep secret in my family for generations. Because we knew ourselves to be beasts, we have always tried to be more than human."

He stood and regarded his wife. "I trusted you with the thing most hidden in my heart and you proved unworthy. I should have known better."

Conan got up from his chair and threw his arms around Paynel. "You are my loyal servant in both your forms. How many rulers can boast of such a thing? Welcome home!"

The next morning Catherine, Hubert and the merchants continued their journey to Rennes. The sun pierced the mist and made the air sparkle and it seemed to Catherine that korrigans and fairies were peeking out at her from behind the trees. Already the adventure was beginning to seem like a fable, something she had been told rather than experienced.

And yet, tied up in her sleeve was a small silver ring, with a rough amethyst, a gift from a knight who was grateful that she had seen the man inside the beast.

(As for Lantilde, she and her husband were exiled to Ireland. It was rumored that they had several children, all born without noses.)

Conventual Spirit

This is the first story I wrote about Catherine in the convent and it takes place before the start of the series. As can be seen, Catherine didn't fit in with the nuns in Brittany and finally settled as a student at the Paraclete. I was asked to write it for Malice Domestic 5, *edited by Elizabeth Foxwell and introduced by Phyllis Whitney from Pocket Books, 1996. There wasn't any particular event in history that prompted it. I just wanted to explore life within a convent.*

———

June 1137, The convent of the Paraclete, Champagne.

"Pride, Catherine. Evil, wicked pride. It will be your damnation, girl!"

Sister Bertrada glared at Catherine, their faces not an inch apart. "You'll never be allowed to become one of us unless you learn some humility," the old nun continued. "How dare you try to lecture me on the blessed St. Jerome! Has some angel sent you a revelation of the Truth?"

Catherine bit her tongue to keep from repeating the argument. She *knew* Sister Bertrada was mistaken.

"No, Sister," she said instead.

Even those two words sounded impudent to Sister Bertrada, who considered the students and novices under her wing to be her own private purgatory. And Catherine Levendeur, with her ready tongue and sharp mind, was her special bane.

"Abbess Heloise has a soft spot for you, though I can't see why." Bertrada shook her head. "I don't find your glib attempts at rhetoric endearing at all."

"No, Sister." Catherine tried to back away, but Sister Bertrada had her wedged into a corner of the refectory and there was no farther back to go.

"What you need is some serious manual labor."

Catherine stifled a groan. Sister Bertrada did not consider sitting for hours hunched over a table laboriously copying a Psalter to be real work. Never mind that her fingers cramped, her back ached, and her eyes burned at the end of the day. However, she tried to look meek and obliging as she awaited the orders of her superior.

She succeeded about as well as most sixteen-year-old girls would.

Sister Bertrada had eyes like the Archangel Michael which glowed with righteousness and ferreted out the most deeply hidden sins. Her cane tapped the wooden floor with ominous thumps as she considered an appropriate penance.

"Go find Sister Felicitia," she told Catherine at last. "Ask her to give you a bucket and a brush. The transept of the oratory has mud all over the floor. You can easily finish it before Vespers if you give the work the same passion you use to defy me."

Catherine bowed her head, hopefully in outward submission. Sister Bertrada snorted to show that she wasn't fooled in the least, turned and marched out, leaving Catherine once again defeated by spiritual authority.

Outside she was met by her friend and fellow student, Emilie. Emilie took one look at Catherine's face and started laughing.

"Why in the world did you feel you had to tell Sister Bertrada that St. Jerome nagged poor St. Paula to death?"

Catherine shrugged. "I was only quoting from a letter of St. Ambrose. I thought it was interesting that even those holy people had their quarrels."

Emilie shook her head in wonder. "You've been here a year and you still have no sense about when to speak and when to keep silent. Sister Melisande would find it amusing, as would Mother Heloise, but Sister Bertrada . . . !"

"I agree," Catherine said sadly. "And now I'm to pay for it on my knees, as usual."

"And proper." Emilie smiled at her fondly. "Oh, Catherine, you do make lessons interesting, if more volatile. I'm so glad you came here."

Catherine sighed. "So am I. Now if only Sister Bertrada could share our happiness."

If meekness were the only test for judging the worthiness of a soul, then Sister Felicitia should have inherited the earth long ago. She was the only daughter of a noble family who ought to have had to do nothing more than sing the hours, sew, and copy manuscripts. Her only distinction was that her face was marred by deep scars running across her cheeks from temple to jaw. Catherine had never heard how she came by them, but assumed that this disfigurement was the reason she was in the convent instead of married to some lord. Although for the dowry Felicitia commanded, it was surprising that no one was willing to take her, no matter what she looked like.

Felicitia certainly didn't behave like a pampered noblewoman. She always volunteered when the most disagreeable tasks were assigned, things even the lay sisters dreaded doing. She scrubbed out the reredorter, even leaning into the holes in the seats above the river to scrub the filth from the inside. She hauled wood and dug vegetables. She never lifted her eyes from the job she was given, never raised her voice in dispute.

Catherine didn't know what to make of her.

"I'll need the bucket later this evening," Sister Felicitia said when Catherine stated her orders. "I'd help you, of course, but I'm dyeing today."

Catherine had noticed. The woman's hands were stained blue with woad. It would be days before it all washed off. Sister Felicitia didn't appear concerned by this. Nor did she seem aware that the day was soft and bright and that the other nuns were all sitting in the cloister, sewing and chatting softly while soaking up the June sunshine.

"Sister Bertrada wants me to do this alone, anyway," Catherine said, picking up the bucket and brush. Sister Felicitia nodded without looking up. She did not indulge in unnecessary conversation.

Catherine spilled half the water tripping over the doorstop to the oratory. Coming in from the sunlight, it seemed to her that there were bright doves fluttering before her eyes. Watching them, she missed the step in the darkness, and then mopped up the puddles before spending the better part of the afternoon scrubbing the stone floor. But, true to Sister Bertrada's prediction, she did indeed have the job finished in time for Vespers, although her robes were still damp and stained at the hem, unsuitable attire for the Divine Office.

And that was how she knew there had been no muddy footprints on the oratory floor when the nuns retired to the dormitory that evening.

Of course, Sister Bertrada didn't believe her.

"This time, do it properly," she told Catherine as she handed her the bucket the next day.

Catherine fervently wanted to protest. She had scrubbed the floor thoroughly, half of it with her own skirts. It had been clean. Perhaps one of the nuns had forgotten and worn her wooden clogs to prayers instead of her slippers. It wasn't her fault.

But Catherine knew that she would never be allowed to remain at the Paraclete if she contradicted Sister Bertrada every time she opened her mouth, and she wanted to stay in the convent more than anything else in the world. So she took the proffered bucket and returned to the dark oratory.

She propped the door open to the light in and knelt to begin the task.

"That's odd," she said as she started on the marks.

"That's *very* odd," she added as she went on to the next ones.

She knew these had to have been made recently, after Compline, when all the women had retired for the night. They were in the shape of footprints, starting at the door and running across the transept to the chapter room, stopping at the bottom of the steps to the nuns' dormitory. The marks were smudged, perhaps by the slippers of the nuns when they came down just before dawn for Vigils and Lauds. But the muddy prints had certainly been made by bare feet. And they were still damp.

Who could have entered the oratory secretly in the middle of the night?

Catherine wondered about it all the while she was scrubbing. When she had finished, she went to the prioress, Astane, for an explanation.

"These footprints," Astane asked. "You already removed them?"

"Sister Bertrada told me to," Catherine explained.

The prioress nodded. "Very good, child. You are learning."

"But I know they weren't there yesterday evening," Catherine insisted. "I did clean the floor carefully the first time. Someone was in the oratory after we went to bed."

"That seems unlikely." Astane did not appear alarmed by Catherine's statement. "The door is barred on the inside, after all."

"Then how did the footprints get there?" Catherine persisted.

The prioress raised her eyebrows. "That is not your concern, my dear."

"It is if I have to wipe them up," Catherine muttered under her breath.

Not far enough under. Astane's hand gripped her chin tightly and tilted her face upward.

"I presume you were praying just then," the prioress said.

Catherine marveled at the strength in these old women. Sister Bertrada, Prioress Astane: they both must be nearly seventy, but with hands as firm and steady as a blacksmith's. And eyes that saw the smallest lie.

"No, Sister," she admitted. "But I am now. *Domine, noli me arguere in ira tua . . .*"

The prioress' lip twitched and her sharp glance softened. "Lord, do not rebuke me in your anger . . ." she translated. "Catherine, dear, I'm not angry with you and I hope and trust that our Lord isn't, either."

She paused. "Sister Bertrada, on the other hand . . ."

Catherine needed no further warning. She resolved not to mention the footprints in the oratory again.

But the next morning, everyone saw them.

The light of early dawn slanted through the narrow windows of the chapter, illuminating the clumps of damp earth, a few fresh stalks still clinging to them, forming a clear trail of footprints across the room.

"How did those get there?" Emilie whispered to Catherine, peering down the stairs over the shoulders of the choir nuns.

"They're exactly the same as yesterday," Catherine whispered back. "But I'm sure I cleaned it all. I know I did."

Sister Bertrada and Sister Felicitia walked through the marks, apparently without noticing, but the other women stopped. They look at each other in confusion, pointing at the footprints that started at the barred door to the garden, went through the oratory and ended at the steps to their sleeping room.

Sister Ursula shuddered. "Something is coming for us!" she shrieked. "A wild man of the woods has invaded the convent!"

A few of the others gave startled cries, but Emilie giggled, putting a hand over her mouth to stifle the sound. Behind her, Sister Bietriz bent closer.

"What is it?" she whispered.

Emilie swallowed her mirth. 'Wild man' indeed!" she said softly. "Maybe Sister Bertrada has a secret lover!"

Catherine and Bietriz exploded in unseemly laughter. Emilie joined in.

"*Quiet!*" The object of their speculation raised her cane in warning.

They composed themselves as quickly as possible, knowing that the matter would not be forgotten, but hoping to alleviate the punishment with a return to good behavior.

It was not to be.

"Catherine," Sister Bertrada went on. "Since you and Emilie find this mess so amusing, you may clean it up. Bietriz, you shall help them."

Catherine opened her mouth to object that she had already removed the marks but they had only returned. Just as she inhaled to speak, Emilie stepped on her toe.

"Yie . . . yes, Sister," Catherine said.

Privately, she agreed with both Ursula and Emilie. The marks must have been made by a wild man of the forest. For who else could become enamored of Sister Bertrada?

"You're right, there is something very strange about this," Emilie told Catherine as they scrubbed. "Who could be getting in every night? And why doesn't Mother Heloise say something about it? Do you think she knows who it is?"

Catherine wrung out the mop. Bietriz, whose family was too exalted for floor duty, leaned against the wall and pointed out spots they missed.

"Mother Heloise probably doesn't think this is worth commenting on," she said. "Perhaps she thinks someone is playing a trick and doesn't want them encouraged. You don't really believe one of us is letting a man in, do you?"

"Who?" Emilie asked. "Sister Bertrada? She and Sister Felicitia would be the most logical suspects. Since they sleep on either side of the door, they have the best chance of leaving at night without being noticed."

Catherine tried to imagine either woman tiptoeing down the steps to let in a secret lover. In Sister Bertrada's case her imagination couldn't stretch far enough.

She laughed. "I find it easier to believe in a monster."

"It's not that preposterous," Emile considered. "Sister Felicitia is really quite beautiful, even now. I've heard that she had a number of men eager to marry her, but she refused them all. Her father was furious when she announced that she would only wed Our Lord."

Catherine leaned back on her heels and thought about this. "I suppose she might have changed her mind," she said. "Perhaps one of her suitors continued to pursue her even here and convinced her that he wanted her despite her scars."

Beatriz shook her head. "I don't think so, Catherine. Felicitia made those scars herself, with the knife she used to cut embroidery thread. She sliced right through her cheeks, purposely, so that no one would desire her. That was how her father was finally convinced to let her come here."

Catherine sat back in shock, knocking over the bucket of soapy water.

"How do you know this?" she asked.

"It was common knowledge at the time," Bietriz answered. "I was about twelve then. I remember how upset my mother was about it. Felicitia threatened to cut off her own nose next. It's dreadful to say, but I benefited from her example. When I announced that I wanted to come to the Paraclete, no one dared oppose me. Mother even refused to let me have my sewing basket unless she was in the room, just in case."

"I see." Catherine was once again reminded that she was only a merchant's daughter, at the convent by virtue of her quick mind and her father's money. Bietriz came from one of the best families in Champagne, related in some way even to the count. She knew all about the life of a noblewoman and all the gossip that Catherine would not normally be privy to. At the Paraclete they could be sisters in Christ, but not in the world.

"Very well," Catherine conceded. "I will accept that Sister Felicitia is not likely to be letting a lover in. But I don't see how any of the rest of us could do it without waking anyone."

"Nor do I," Emilie agreed. "In which case we might have to consider Ursula's theory."

"That some half-human creature came in from the forest?" Catherine snorted.

Emilie stood, shaking out her skirts. Beatriz picked up the bucket, her contribution to the labor.

"Of course not," Emilie said. "Even a half-human monster would have to unbar the door from the inside. But Satan can pass through bars and locks, if someone summons him. And it's said that he often appears as a beautiful young man."

Bietriz was skeptical. "So we should demand to know who has been having dreams of passionate seduction lately? Who would admit to that?"

Catherine felt a chill run down her pine. Was it possible that one of them could be inviting Evil into the convent, perhaps unwittingly? It was well known that the devil used dreams to lure and confuse the innocent into consenting to sin. She tried to remember her dreams of the past few nights. The memories were dim, so it was likely that they only came from *ventris inanitate*, deriving from an empty stomach and of no consequence.

They walked out into the sunlight and Catherine felt the fear diminish. While it was true that Satan used dreams to tempt weak humans, sin could occur only when one was awake. Tertullian said so and Catherine agreed. We can no more be condemned for dreaming we are sinners than rewarded for dreaming we are saints.

"And why should the devil leave footprints?" She continued the thought aloud. "That doesn't seem very subtle."

Emilie didn't want to give up her demon lover theory.

"There is a rock near my home with a dent in it that everyone says is the devil's toe print," she told Catherine. "So why not the whole foot? Satan is known to be devious. Perhaps he doesn't want to trap one soul. He may be trying to sow dissension among us so that he may take us all."

Bietriz had moved on to another worry. "Why is it that the feet only come in?" she asked them. "How does the intruder get out?"

"Perhaps he turns into something else," Emilie speculated happily. "Satan can do that too, you know."

She seemed delighted with her conclusions, and her expression dared them to come up with a refutation.

Catherine looked at her carefully. Was she serious? Did she really believe they were being visited by the devil as shape-changer? Emilie was usually scornful of such tales. Why was she so eager to assign a supernatural explanation to this?

An answer leaped unbidden to her mind.

Emilie's bed wasn't that far from the door.

Catherine tried to suppress the thought as unworthy, but it wouldn't stay down.

Emilie was blonde, beautiful, and also from a noble family. Perhaps she wasn't as happy in the convent as she pretended. It entailed a much smaller stretch of the imagination to see Emilie unbarring the door for a lover than Sister Felicitia.

But that explanation didn't satisfy her, either. It wasn't like Emilie. And Catherine was sure Mother Heloise and Prioress Astane didn't believe that one of the nuns had a secret lover, human or demon. If they did, then Brother Baldwin and the other lay brothers who lived nearby would have been set to guard the oratory entrance.

She was missing something. Catherine hated to leave a puzzle unsolved. She had to find out who was doing this. She sighed. It was either that or spend the rest of her life scrubbing the oratory floor.

It was nearly midsummer. The days were long and busy. Apart from reciting the Divine Office seven times a day, the nuns all performed manual labor. They studied, copied manuscripts for the convent library, sewed both church vestments and their own clothing as well as doing the daily round of cleaning, cooking and gardening necessary to keep themselves alive.

Catherine meant to stay awake that night but, after the long day, she fell asleep as soon as she lay down and didn't wake until the bell rang for Vigils.

Even in the dim light of the lamp carried by Sister Felicitia, they could all see the fresh footprints at the bottom of the stairs.

Sister Ursula retreated to the top of the steps whimpering and had to be ordered by Sister Bertrada to continue to the oratory. The others obeyed as well. Bertrada's cane was more frightening than unseen demons. But their reluctance was obvious.

Mother Heloise and Prioress Astane were already waiting in the chapel. Their presence reassured the women and reminded them of their duty of prayer. However, Catherine was not the only one who looked to see if the bar was still across the garden door.

"Satan won't distract me," Emilie whispered virtuously. "He can't get you while you're praying."

Catherine wasn't so confident. Whatever was doing this had thoroughly distracted her. She missed the antiphon more than once and knew that bowing her apology to God would not save her from Sister Bertrada's rebuke.

There had to be an explanation for this, either natural or supernatural. Catherine did care which it was. She only wanted to discover the truth.

The next day was the eve of the feast of the Nativity of St. John the Baptist.

There would be a special vigil that night. It was also midsummer's eve, a time of spirits crossing between worlds, a fearsome long twilight. A good Christian could be driven mad or worse by the things that walked this night. These ideas were officially denied and forbidden by church doctrine, but children learned the folk tales before they were weaned and such deep beliefs are hard to uproot. Even the shimmering sunlight of the summer morning was not bright enough to dispel the shadows of the mind.

Each afternoon while they worked in the cloister, the women were permitted some edifying conversation. Today, the usual gentle murmurs and soft laughter had become a buzzing of wonderment, anger and fear.

"What if tonight this thing doesn't stop at the bottom of the stairs?" Sister Ursula said, her eyes round with terror and anticipation. "What if it climbs right up and into our beds?"

"All of ours, or just yours?" Bietriz asked.

Ursula reddened with anger. "What are you implying?" she demanded "I would never bring scandal upon us! How dare you even suggest such a thing?"

Bietriz sighed and put down her sewing. She went over to Ursula and took her gently by the shoulders.

"I apologize," she said. "It was not a kind joke. I make no accusations. I believe, though, that you have become overwrought by these happenings. Perhaps you should sleep with Sister Melisande in the infirmary tonight."

"Perhaps I shall," Ursula muttered. "Better than being slandered by my sisters or murdered by demons in the dortor."

Sister Felicitia was seated on the grass, her stained hands weaving softened reeds to mend a basket. She looked up.

"There are no demons here," she said firmly.

They all stared at her. It would have been more surprising if a sheep in the meadow had suddenly spouted philosophy.

"How do you know?" Ursula asked.

"Mother Heloise promised me," Felicitia answered with perfect certainty. "The demons won't come for me here."

She bent again to her work. The others were silent.

"Well," Ursula said finally, "perhaps I will stay in the dortor. But if anything attacks me, I'll scream so loud you'll think Judgment Day has come."

"If you wake me," Emilie warned, "you'll wish it had."

Before Vespers, Abbess Heloise gathered all the women together in the chapter room. There was a collective sigh of relief as they assembled. Finally, all would be explained.

The abbess smiled at them all fondly. Her large brown eyes studied them, and Catherine felt that Mother Heloise knew just what each of them was thinking and feeling.

"It has been brought to my attention," she began, "that some of you have been concerned about mud stains in the oratory and chapel. I fear you have allowed your speculations to go beyond normal curiosity. This has led to unwholesome suspicion. It saddens me greatly. If something so natural and common as wet earth can cause you to imagine demons and suspect each other of immoral behavior, then I have not done my duty as your mentor or your mother."

There was a rustle of surprise and denial. Heloise held up her hand for silence. There was silence.

"Therefore," she continued. "I apologize to you all for not providing the proper spiritual guidance. I will endeavor to do so in the future and will ask our founder, Master Abelard, for advice on how this may best be done. I hope you will forgive me."

That was all. Heloise signaled the chantress to lead them in for Vespers.

They followed in bewildered obedience. Catherine and Emilie stared at each other, shaking their heads. As far as Catherine could understand, they had just been told that the intruder in the convent was none of their business. It made no sense.

Mindful of her earlier mistakes, Catherine tried desperately to keep her attention on the service for St. John's Eve, despite the turmoil in her mind.

"*Ecce, mitto angelum meum . . .*" Behold, I send my angel who will prepare the way for you before my coming. "*Vox clamantis in deserto . . .*" A voice crying in the wilderness.

She tried to concentrate on St. John. It was hard to imagine him as a baby, leaping for joy in his mother's womb when they visited the Virgin Mary. Instead, she always saw him as the gaunt man of the desert, living naked on a diet of locusts and honey. People must have thought him mad, preaching the coming of a savior.

Ecce, mitto angelum meum . . .

All at once Catherine realized what she had been doing wrong. She had been examining the problem from one direction only. Mother Heloise knew the answer. That's why she wasn't worried. When one turned the proposition around it made perfect sense. Now, if only she could stay awake tonight to prove her theory.

The summer night, usually too brief, seemed to stretch on forever. Catherine was beginning to think that she had made an error in her logic.

At last there was a rustling from the other end of the room. Someone was getting up. Catherine waited. Whoever it was could be coming her way, to use the reredortor. No one passed her bed. She heard a faint creak from the far end of the room as if someone else were awake. Peering over the sheet, she saw nothing but dim shapes. There were no more noises. Perhaps it had only been someone tossing about in a nightmare.

Carefully, Catherine eased out of bed. All the nuns and students slept fully dressed, even to their slippers, so as to be ready for the Night Office. Catherine looked up and down the rows of beds on either side of the room. Everyone seemed to be accounted for and asleep. Slowly, fearing even to breathe, Catherine moved down the room to the door to the Chapter. It was wide open.

All the tales of monsters and demons came rushing suddenly into her mind. Anything could be at the foot of those steps. Who would protect her if she encountered them against orders, because of her arrogant curiosity?

She said a quick prayer to St. Catherine of Alexandria, who had also wondered about things, and started down the stairs.

When she reached the bottom, Catherine nearly fainted in terror as she stepped onto a pile of something soft that moved under her foot. Shaking, she made herself bend down and touch it.

It was clothing just like her own: a shift, a long tunic, a belt and a pair of slippers. The discovery of something so familiar and yet so out of place terrified Catherine even more.

What had happened to the woman who had worn these clothes?

Moonlight shone through the open door of the oratory. Catherine looked down at the floor. In her panic, she had almost forgotten to test her conclusion.

She was right. The floor was clean. So far, nothing had entered. Feeling a little more confident, she stepped out into the midsummer night.

The herb garden lay tranquil under the moon. Catherine had been out there once before at night, helping Sister Melisande pick the plants that were most potent when gathered at the new moon. This time she was here uninvited.

There was a break in the hedge on the other side of the garden. Catherine thought she saw a flicker of something white in the grove just beyond. Before she could consider the stupidity of her actions, she hurried toward it.

Within the grove there was a small hill that was free of both trees and undergrowth. Sheep grazed there by day, but tonight . . . *Ecce, mitto angelum!*

Catherine stopped at the edge of the trees. There was someone on the hill, pale skin glowing silver in the moonlight, golden curls surrounding her face like a halo. It was Sister Felicitia, naked, dancing in the night, her feet spattered with mud. Her arms were raised as she spun, her face to the sky, her back arched, moving to some music that Catherine couldn't hear.

A hand touched her shoulder. Catherine gasped and the hand moved to cover her mouth.

"Make no sound," Abbess Heloise warned. "You'll wake her."

Catherine nodded and Heloise removed her hand.

"How did you find out?" the abbess asked quietly.

"It was the footprints," Catherine whispered back, not taking her eyes off Felicitia. "We all thought they were from someone being let in. But it made much more sense if they were made by someone coming back. Then there didn't need to be an intruder. Anyone can open the door from the inside. What I didn't understand were the prints of bare feet."

"She always leaves her robes at the bottom of the stairs and puts them on again before returning to bed," Heloise explained.

"But shouldn't we stop her?" Catherine asked. "She must be possessed to behave like this."

"She might be," Heloise admitted. "I worried about that, too. But Sister Bertrada convinced me that, if she is, it's by nothing evil and we have no right to interfere."

"Sister Bertrada?" Catherine's voice raised in astonishment.

"Hush!" Heloise said. "Yes, Bertrada is on the other side of the grove, watching to be sure no one interrupts. Brother Baldwin is farther on, guarding the gate to the road. Not everyone who saw her would understand. Do you?"

Catherine shook her head. She didn't understand, but it didn't matter. She was only grateful that she had been allowed to watch. Felicitia, dancing in the moonlight, wasn't licentious, but sublime. She shone like Eve on the first morning, radiant with delight at the wonder of Eden, in blissful ignorance of sin. The joy of it made Catherine weep in her own knowledge that soon the serpent would come and, with it, sorrow.

Heloise guided Catherine away gently.

"She'll finish soon and go back to bed," the abbess explained. "Sister Bertrada will see that she gets there safely. Come with me. Astane has left some warm cider for me. You may have a cup also, before you go back."

When they were settled in Heloise's room, drinking the herbed cider, Catherine finally asked the question.

"I figured out who and how, Mother," she said. "But I still don't understand why."

Heloise gazed into her cider bowl for several minutes. Catherine thought she might not answer. Perhaps the abbess didn't know.

At last she appeared to come to a decision.

"Catherine," she asked, "have you ever believed that you were loved by no one, that you were completely alone?"

Catherine thought. "Well," she answered. "There was about a month when I was thirteen, but . . . no, no. Even then I always knew my family loved me. I know you love me. I know God loves me, unworthy though I am of all of you."

Heloise smiled, relaxing. "That's right, on all points. But until she came here, Felicitia believed that no one loved her, that God had abandoned her; and she had reason. That is not a story for you to hear. I only want you to understand that I am sure Felicitia is not possessed by anything evil."

"I believe you," Catherine said. "But I still don't understand why she dances in her sleep."

"I didn't either," Heloise admitted, "until Sister Bertrada explained it to me. Don't make such a face, child, child. Bertrada sees further into you heart than you know."

"That doesn't comfort me, Mother."

"It should." Heloise leaned over and patted Catherine's knee. "Bertrada told me that Felicitia spent her whole life being desired for her beauty, her wealth and her family connections. In all that desire, there was no love. Often there was unconscionable abuse. So she felt that she wasn't worthy of love and consented to despair. She endured much to find her way to us. The scars on her face are mild compared to the ones on her soul. She struggles every day with demons worse than any Sister Ursula can imagine. And, until a week ago, she had nightmares almost every night."

"And then . . ." Catherine was enthralled by the tale.

"And then," Heloise smiled again. "Joy came to her one night, and she went to the garden and danced. It has only been in her sleep so far, but if she is left in peace, we are hoping that soon she will also have joy in the morning, all through the day and, at last, be healed."

Catherine sat for a long while, until the cider went cold and the chantress rose to ring the bell for Vigils. Heloise waited patiently.

"Are you satisfied, Catherine?" she asked as they rose to go. "You assembled the evidence, arranged it properly, and solved the mystery. There is no need to tell the others."

"Oh, no, I wouldn't do that," Catherine promised. "I only wanted to know the truth for myself."

"Then why do you look so sad?" Heloise prodded.

"It's only—" Catherine stopped, embarrassed. "I'm so clumsy, Mother. If only I could dance like Felicitia, even in my sleep."

Heloise laughed. "And how do you know you don't?"

For once in her life, Catherine had no reply.

Death Before Compline

I wrote this story by request for Death Dines at 8:30 *edited by Nick DiChario and Claudia Bishop, published by Berkley in 2000. They asked that a meal be part of the plot and that I include a recipe. The first part was easy; I always include food. The second part was more difficult because collections of recipes didn't appear for another couple of hundred years. If your mother didn't teach you, then you usually didn't learn. But I've read enough about meals that I imagined what would be used. I also tried it at home and it appears at the end of this book. For those who have read the series, you know that Margaret is the daughter of Count Thibault's illegitimate daughter. I thought about putting something in about that but decided it would make the story too complicated. But, if you're worried, I promise that Thibault spent time with his granddaughter. Thibault was a real person, the grandson of William the Conqueror. His son, Henry, did go on Crusade.*

Spring 1146: The convent of the Paraclete, Champagne

Catherine sat on a stone step, a basket of grain between her knees. She lazily tossed handfuls in the direction of a flock of chickens who seemed more interested in pecking at her bare toes than in eating their dinner.

Behind her were the walls of the convent of the Paraclete. Once Catherine had thought she would spend all her days behind those walls, but her life had flowed in channels she hadn't expected and now she was able to make only an occasional visit.

The calm of the place refreshed her, as did the fact that many of the nuns and lay sisters were happy to relieve her of her duties to her two small children, James and Edana.

Catherine scattered a last handful of the seeds before she stood, shook out her skirts, and went back into the cloister to be sure that her active progeny weren't wearing out their welcome.

Inside she found not the peace she'd come to expect, but commotion. The nuns and lay sisters were hurrying toward the guest house with bundles of linen, pitchers, and washing bowls.

"What's happening?" she asked.

Sister Cecile paused only a moment. "Company coming," she panted. "Count Thibault, Lord Henry, Lord Milo, their families, retainers. Wherever shall we put them all?"

She dashed on.

Catherine looked around for someone who could give her more information.

Outside the chapter house stood the abbess of the Paraclete, Heloise. Despite the activity around her, the abbess was calm, answering and directing the women who fluttered by her like bees seeking nectar. As each of the sisters received her orders, she sped away.

Catherine hovered on the edge of the group, not sure if she should offer to help now that she was only a visitor to the convent. Heloise noticed her and beckoned her closer.

"You might see to Sister Genevieve," she said. "She's in the chapter now, drawing up our copy of the sale."

"Yes, Mother," Catherine said.

Heloise nodded approval and turned to the next problem.

What sale? Catherine thought as she edged around the others and went into the chapter, the room next to the chapel where the nuns met each week for lectures and work assignments. At a table under a window sat Sister Genevieve, sharpening her reed pen.

Catherine didn't know Genevieve well: she had arrived at the convent after Catherine had left to be married. She was in her mid-twenties, with fair skin and amber eyes. Without having spoken to her, Catherine had formed the impression that she was both competent and devout, if a bit skittish. She tended to start like a frightened colt when caught unawares. As Catherine entered, Genevieve looked up. There was ink at the corner of her mouth. She started to speak but coughed instead. Her cheeks were flushed, as with fever.

"Mother Heloise thought you might be able to use my help," Catherine told her.

Genevieve's forehead wrinkled. "I can't imagine why," she said, her voice hoarse. "I'm simply making a list of the land Lord Milo is selling us the use of to pay for his pilgrimage to the Holy Land. I'm not too ill to do this."

"Lord Milo's going on the expedition, as well?" Catherine remarked. She supposed it shouldn't surprise her. It seemed that everyone from King Louis down to the beggars in the road were taking the cross.

"But why are we buying the tithe from him?" she asked. "With what? It was Lord Milo who gave the land for the Paraclete in the first place. Have we become rich since I was here?"

Genevieve shrugged. "That's Mother Heloise's affair. My job is to itemize the various properties so that we have our own record, as well as the charter drawn up by Lord Milo's clerk."

Catherine came around her to see what had already been written. One glance told her why the abbess had wanted someone else to assist the nun. Genevieve wrote a good clear hand and her Latin was excellent, but she appeared to have no sense of geography.

"You can't mean this," Catherine said tactlessly, pointing to a line. "These boundaries would give us a field three miles long and only a hand-breadth wide. Why would we want the verge of a road?"

Genevieve coughed repeatedly as she looked at the words. "That's what is written on the tablet that Lord Milo's clerk gave me."

She handed it to Catherine, who studied the abbreviated words scrawled in the warm wax. Genevieve was right.

"Then the clerk must have made a mistake," she said. "I'll ask Mother Heloise about it."

Genevieve jerked the tablet away. "I can ask her myself, thank you," she snapped. "You might remember, Catherine, that you're but a guest here. You had your chance to stay but you rejected God for the life of the flesh. So don't try to wiggle back in, especially when the evidence of your lust is so obvious."

Catherine was taken aback. It was a moment before she realized that Genevieve was talking about James and Edana. She supposed that her children would be considered proof that her marriage had been con-summated and she couldn't deny that se was always more than happy to do her wifely duty, but . . .

"What has that to do with an error in computation?" she asked.

Genevieve didn't answer. She bent to her work once again, blunting the reed tip with the pressure she put on the parchment. Her coughing was strong enough to cause her to blot the page.

"Could I get you a posset to ease your cough?" Catherine regretted her uninvited criticism.

"Sister Melisande gave me a syrup, thank you." Genevieve didn't look up.

Catherine was dismissed.

She wished that her husband, Edgar, were here so that she could relieve her indignation by telling him. But Edgar had gone to see about arranging for the care of some horses that they were buying from a Spanish merchant and selling at the fair at Troyes. He wouldn't be back until the end of the week.

Checking to see that Sister Jehanne wasn't being worn out by her children, Catherine found the nun, the baby and Edgar's sister, Margaret, washing clothes. The room was steamy, but Catherine made out the strong arms of Sister Jehanne as she lifted the soaking cloth from the hot water and into the cold to rinse. Margaret had a long paddle to push the cloth under the water. Out of the way in the corner baby Edana was sitting naked on a pile of what Catherine devoutly hoped were soiled robes. James was trotting back and forth, handing the nun new pieces to push into the cauldron.

"You could help Margaret, I suppose," Sister Jehanne answered her offer. "But the other paddle seems to have disappeared. Don't worry. We're almost finished anyway. The children have been very helpful."

Since they all seemed quite happy with what they were doing, Catherine went to the guest house to see if she could be of use there.

"No, no, dear," the portress, Sister Thecla assured her. "Only Lady Isabel and her maid will be staying with us. We can handle that. Count Thibault and Lord Milo are bringing tents for the men. But we'll have to get them all at least one good meal and I have no idea how that would be managed."

Cooking wasn't one of Catherine's accomplishments. In Paris they either had their own cook or they bought something at one of the bakeshops. She decided not to offer her services in the kitchen.

Without the children or the running of a household to occupy her, Catherine realized that she didn't know what to do with herself. The only thing that appealed was to go back to the chapter house to read, but having to see Sister Genevieve again was more than she could tolerate.

Finally, she made her way to the abbess' room, where Heloise sat alone, having at last finished giving the sisters their assignments.

"Mother?" Catherine instantly regretted interrupting. Heloise sat at her table, her head bowed in prayer.

At once the head came up. Heloise smiled and rubbed her eyes.

"Forgive me!" she exclaimed. "I must have dozed a moment. Yes, Catherine? Did you finish helping Sister Genevieve?"

Catherine told the abbess of Genevieve's reception of her offer.

"Oh dear." Heloise shook her head. "It's not anything you've done, my dear. Genevieve is upset by our visitors. She's related to Count Milo, you know. There was some fuss about her entering the Paraclete. Her family wanted her to go to Tart, to be closer to them. I fear she's always resented the fact that he sided with them. I pray that someday she'll be able to forgive them all and be at peace."

Catherine's feelings were somewhat assuaged by Heloise's explanation. Perhaps Genevieve felt that the rights Count Milo was selling the nuns should have been donated freely.

Since she was not needed anywhere, Catherine wandered out the gates of the convent to watch for the visitors. She was standing outside the guest house when she spotted the procession coming north up the dusty road.

Shading her eyes with her hand, she watched the riders approach, first Count Thibault and his son, Henry, on fine destriers, and the others behind riding palfreys or leading pack mules. They carried banners with the standard of Champagne and the pilgrim's cross, to proclaim the vow Henry had taken to fight in the Holy Land.

Catherine was so caught up in watching them that she didn't notice the smaller group coming from the opposite direction until she was startled by the hot breath of a horse blowing on her neck and a rough voice shouting.

"You! Girl! What do you think you're doing standing gaping in the road?"

Catherine looked up. She didn't know the man who spoke. He was about her own age, with light eyes and hair the color of unpolished brass. She was about to answer angrily when Sister Thecla came out of the gate, followed by several of the lay brothers of the convent.

"Welcome!" she cried to them all. "Welcome to the Paraclete. My lord count, Lord Milo, we're honored to have you here. The brothers will show you the best places for your tents. Be careful, the land is marshy near the river."

Count Thibault rode up to her and dismounted.

"Sister Thecla," he beamed. "Always good to see you."

He looked past Catherine, then focused on her.

"By the Magdalene's tangled hair!" he exclaimed. "It's Hubert's girl. Catherine, isn't it?"

Catherine went scarlet with mortification. She had hoped no one would spot her until she could return to the guesthouse and change into proper clothes. She bowed to the count, trying to stoop to hide her naked feet.

"My father will be sorry to have missed you," she murmured.

"Not at all," Thibault said. "I saw him in Troyes. He sent some casks of wine on ahead. Have they arrived?"

Sister Thecla nodded. "Yesterday morning," she said. "We thank you for providing them."

"We'll open one tonight for dinner." The count laughed. "See that the ladies in the cloister get a cup each as well."

As the visitors were led either into the guest house or out to the field, Catherine slipped away as unobtrusively as possible. She prayed that her husband and father would never learn that she had been taken for a kitchen maid by some rude lordling, but knew that prayer would not likely be granted. The best she could do was bedeck herself so elegantly that evening that no one would remember her earlier state.

In her room, Catherine rummaged through the packs to find a pair of clean hose and a head scarf. She put these on and laced up her shoes. From the guest-house window she could see the men loading a huge barrel cask onto a platform next to the area where tables were being set up for the banquet. She frowned. With that much wine on hand, perhaps it would be better if the children slept somewhere further from the party. The singing alone would keep them awake, and while Count Thibault and Lord Milo were good, pious men, there were a number of young bachelors in the company. The sort of antics they enjoyed after an evening of barely diluted wine was not something she wanted James imitating.

Four of these young men had gathered under the window. She didn't recognize any of them but there was a slight resemblance to Lord Milo in all. Their heads moved closer together as they spoke; Catherine could hear nothing of the conversation, although from the waving arms, the discussion appeared to be intense. Soon the voices rose so that she could make out the words.

"Roric knows there's nothing he can do," said the man who had yelled at her. "He's been excommunicated. That's why he didn't even bother to come."

"What, again?" One of the others laughed. "I knew he was in for trouble when he started fornication with the bishop's concubine."

"What of it?" another said. "He's never let excommunication bother him before. He'll repent for Easter, as always. Earlier, if he tires of her."

"Stephan is right; Roric will be here," the fourth grumbled. "He'll show up at the worst possible moment, as always. Wait and see."

The others nodded glum agreement. Then the men wandered off toward the tents.

As Catherine looked in her hand mirror to check for stray curls escaping from her scarf, she wondered idly who this Roric was who put the desires of the flesh above the safety of his soul, or of his body, depending on the temperament of the bishop. But then she returned to her primary concern and headed for the infirmary to ask Sister Melisande to keep the children safe there for the night. She only hoped there would be no unexpected patients.

Much later, properly attired and wearing her best pearl earrings, Catherine was presented to Lord Milo; his daughter, Isobel; her husband, Girard; and then the line of men she had seen from the window — Freer, Joiffroy, Gaucher and Stephen, Milo's nephews. Gaucher, it turned out, was the copper-haired man who had yelled at her in the road.

He bowed over her hand with an amused expression.

"I beg your forgiveness, kind lady, for not seeing your true station beneath the dust."

"Perhaps the sun was in your eyes," Catherine answered. She was about to say more, but checked her tongue at a warning glance from Abbess Heloise.

Gaucher stepped back with a polite grimace and they all made their way in for Vespers.

From behind the screen the voices of the nuns rose clear and pure. Catherine forgot her petty irritation in the beauty of the music. The others, too, seemed entranced by the singing of the psalms and stood quietly until the end.

Or did they? From the corner of her eye, Catherine thought she saw a movement as if someone had opened the door. She tried to look without turning, but could see no one. Was it someone arriving late or a music hater trying to slip out? She couldn't tell.

The meal that night was fish, caught in the trap set in the Ardusson River and made into a thick stew with dried fruit and herbs. There was bread and egg soup with fresh greens. Later there would be more fruit, dipped in honey and walnuts. Catherine knew that such a feast was as much as the nuns ate in a week but abstinence indeed for the nobles, who gorged on meat every night if they could, and complained of deprivation on fast days.

A cheer went up as Count Thibault's *pincerna* drove a spout into the wine cask and held a pitcher beneath. The wine flowed for several seconds and then stopped. The servant shook the spout, then signaled to one of the men to tip the cask.

"It's full, I'm sure," one man said. "It was so heavy when we put it up here that I thought we'd drop and spill it."

When the pitcher was full, the wine steward offered the first cup to Abbess Heloise. She let him put a small amount and then filled the cup with water. Next, the count and his son were served. When all the cups were full, Thibault lifted his to drink to the safety of those about to depart for the Holy Land. He took a huge gulp and choked, spraying wine across the table and down his tunic.

"Saint Vincent's rusty pruning hook!" he shouted. "This can't be my wine. It tastes as though it's been strained through a sheep!"

Catherine had done no more than smell the wine before quickly setting the cup down. Thibault ordered his men to pry open the top of the cask. Lord Milo made a joke about the possible contents. His son-in-law and nephews all laughed. As the lid came up, Catherine thought that there was indeed wine enough. It splashed over the men. Then one of then reached over and pulled out something floating on the top.

"Well, that explains it," Count Thibault said. "One of the vintners dropped his hood in the cask. I thought I tasted raw wool. Disgusting."

But the servant was still poking in the wine. Suddenly, he gave a shriek of terror and leapt from the platform. He crossed himself repeatedly and then began frantically wiping his hands on his tunic.

"Holy Mother!" he said over and over. "Blessed Virgin, protect me!"

"What's wrong with the man?" Count Thibault had risen and was striding to the platform, Heloise and Lord Milo close behind him.

"My lord count, my lady abbess," the servant babbled. "You mustn't look!"

By now everyone was gathered around the platform as the count climbed up to the cask. He took one look and blanched. Quickly, he motioned for Abbess Heloise to stay back. Ignoring him, Heloise gazed down into the wine. A face gazed back at her, the eyes wide with shock. She realized that the head floated so easily on the surface because it was no longer attached to a body. Beside it a hand bobbed up, fingers splayed.

Catherine saw the abbess' expression and pushed through the throng to reach her.

"Mother Heloise," she said. "Let me help you."

"I'm fine," Heloise told her, although she was still pale. "Much better than this poor soul. Does anyone know who he is?"

Lord Milo had climbed up as well. He nodded at the face with more sorrow than shock. "Indeed. This is Roric, my eldest nephew. I should have known that only death would keep him from disputing my decision."

In the pandemonium that followed, Catherine was able to help the abbess down and lead her away. It was a sign of her own shock that Catherine could only speak in platitudes.

"How dreadful!" she said. "Who would do such a thing? And why put the body in a wine cask? Think of the mess in having to cut him up first."

Her brain was starting to work again. "There are a hundred places in the woods where the poor man could have been hidden and never discovered. Someone must have wanted his body to be found like this. How wicked! Mother, what should we do?"

Heloise took a deep breath.

"First, Catherine," she said, "we pray for his soul."

"Yes, Mother. Of course." Catherine crossed herself and started a Pater Noster. Then she stopped. "Mother, if the body is Roric, I don't think our prayers will help him. I overheard his brothers saying that Roric is an excommunicate."

For the first time, Heloise's face showed genuine horror.

"Then whoever has committed this awful act has robbed him not only of his life here, but eternally as well." She shook her head in anger. "Catherine, you're right; we must discover this murderer at once."

"But, Mother Heloise," Catherine protested. "Roric may have been killed anywhere and put in the cask at some point between here and Troyes."

"No, Catherine," Heloise said firmly. "You didn't see his face. He couldn't have been in the wine for more than a few hours. His skin wasn't stained at all. Wherever he was killed, he was put in the cask after it arrived here. This is an insult to God and to our order. I intend to get to the bottom of it."

Catherine shuddered, imagining what else might be submerged in the wine.

"But if the man is a nephew of Lord Milo, then it is his responsibility to direct the investigation," she mentioned hesitantly. "Neither he nor Count Thibault may want our advice."

They had entered the cloister now, and were almost at Heloise's room. The abbess stopped and gave Catherine a look of surprise, her eyebrows raised.

"My dear, of course they will," she said firmly. Then her face relaxed into a wicked smile. "Besides, Catherine, when has that ever stopped you before?"

Count Thibault had also realized that the body of Lord Milo's nephew had to have been put in the wine cask after it arrived at the convent. Furthermore, there had only been a few hours, all daylight, between the delivery of the wine and the time the cask had been put on the platform.

"It makes no sense," Milo told the count in his tent that evening. "Putting the body in the wine was a direct attack on you, or me. It's as if Roric was killed only to provide an insult to us."

Thibault didn't want to agree. It would be much simpler if Lord Milo's nephew had been waylaid by bandits on the road. But once they had drained the cask and laid out the body parts, they could find no sign of a death wound. Robbers couldn't have managed to dismember him so neatly. Nor would they have been so foolish as to waste time doing so.

With a sigh, Thibault stood up from his cot.

"We are forced to assume that this hideous deed was committed by someone we know, Milo." He frowned. "And that was done shortly before our arrival here or almost immediately afterward."

Milo didn't look up at the count but fixed his eyes on the ground, strewn with hay and sweet herbs. His hands rested limply on his knees.

"I know that, Thibault," he said. "And I fear that the finger points at someone of my household, even of my blood."

"It has been said that Roric opposed the sale of the tithes to the nuns," Thibault continued. "By what right did he claim them?"

"Roric insisted that the land at Charmes up to the mill was part of his mother's, my sister's, dower," Milo answered. "It was. But before she died, she told all of us that the nuns were eventually to be given the use of it to help feed and clothe her daughter, Genevieve, who is a member of their order. The other boys agreed."

He opened the tent flap. "The land is so close that it's possible to see the mill from here, even in twilight."

Thibault followed him out.

"Hardly worth killing a man for," he commented.

"Only Roric wanted it," Milo added. "I can't imagine the abbess wielding an ax on a man for a bit of land."

Thibault snorted at the image of petite Heloise with any weapon.

Milo continued. "No, I believe we should look for someone with a grudge against us. I fear poor Roric was nothing more than a convenient victim."

The next morning Catherine consulted with the abbess as soon as the morning office had been sung.

"Someone has started a rumor that it was our lay brothers who murdered this man to keep him from contesting his mother's gift," Heloise told her.

"That's nonsense," Catherine exclaimed. "Even if any of the brothers were capable of such evil, why arrange for the body to be so publicly found?"

"I didn't say it was logical, Catherine," Heloise answered. "Rumor hardly ever is. But that won't keep people from believing it."

"Would Roric have demanded more money from the convent for the use of the land?" Catherine asked.

Heloise smiled. "You fear we couldn't have paid? Don't worry, my child. Lord Henry gave us five hundred *livres* of Troyes to pray for his soul while he's in the Holy Land. There would have been enough to give something to Roric."

Catherine was ashamed of herself for feeling even a shred of doubt. But if she could have suspected someone from the convent, however briefly, then how much more easily would strangers?

"We need to examine the area around where the casks were first stored," Catherine said. "There may be some evidence to tell us how the body got there."

Heloise chook her head. "Count Thibault was out there at first light," she said. "The ground is muddy with dozens of footprints. But there is no sign of spilled blood, or spilled wine, for that matter."

"But, there must be — " Catherine started.

She was interrupted by a small body wrapping itself around her knees.

"Mama." James' hands reached up and tugged at her braid. "Sister Emily said I could come with her to hunt for mushrooms, but you have to say yes. Do you?"

"I thought you were supposed to be watching your little sister." She gave her son a stern look that didn't faze him a bit.

"Sister Genevieve and Aunt Margaret are playing with her," James explained. "Edana isn't any fun. She chews my wooden soldiers. Please let me go with Sister Emily."

"Do you think it's safe?" Catherine asked the abbess.

"Emily knows the paths," Heloise assured her. "They won't go out of hearing distance."

Catherine gave her permission. James loped away in delight at the possibility of adventure in the woods. He was a child who could go hunting for mushrooms and come home with tales of dragons and tree sprites. Sometimes Catherine wondered if he didn't really see marvels everywhere he looked.

Assured that the children were taken care of, she turned her attention back to the matter of murder.

"I told you what I overheard from Lord Milo's other nephews," she said. "They seemed not to know where Roric was, but one of them could have been lying. And they certainly didn't sound very fond of him."

"Disliking someone, especially a brother, is far from the kind of hatred that would allow a person to hack a body into pieces," Heloise reminded her.

"But someone did it, Mother," Catherine argued. "And it's no less preposterous than the idea that he would be murdered for nothing more than the tithes on a strip of road and a mill."

She stopped. "A strip of road . . . Mother Heloise, did Sister Genevieve come to you about an error in the measuring of Lord Milo's land? I read it to say that we only had rights to the verge along the road. Genevieve showed me the wax tablet from the clerk and that's what it said, but that makes no sense."

Heloise rubbed her forehead. "I don't remember the details of the transaction, not with all that has happened. Genevieve didn't come to me, but she probably forgot all about it once she heard her brother had been murdered."

"Brother!" Catherine hadn't known that. "Oh, poor Genevieve. Well, all I can think is that one of Lord Milo's nephews must have arrived here before the others and killed his brother. But why? And why put him in the wine?"

They were interrupted again by the sound of Sister Emily shouting.

"James!" she was calling. "James, bring that to me at once!"

"What's he done now?" Catherine ran to find her son.

James was dashing through the open gate, carrying a long piece of wood. He waved it around his head and made as if to tilt at an imaginary foe. Instead he ran headlong into his mother.

"Naughty boy!" She held him with one hand and took away the board with the other. "Didn't you hear Sister Emily? What have you found?"

She knew what it was at once, one of the paddles used in the laundry. Had James taken it with him the day before? The wood, normally pale from hot water and soap, was stained a deep purple. James too was covered in a mixture of mud and what smelled like wine.

Emily hurried to them. "I'm sorry, Catherine. He wandered off from me, hunting for the mushrooms. I don't know how it came to be so wet under the tree. We were well away from the river."

"Did you let him bring the paddle?" Catherine asked.

"No, he found it there."

Catherine lifted James to her hip and rushed back to the abbess. She showed Heloise the paddle and told her where it had been found.

Heloise understood at once.

"It cannot be!" she exclaimed. "And yet, here is the proof."

"Someone else could have taken it outside the convent," Catherine ventured.

"For what reason would it even be outside the laundry?" Heloise said. "We must face the fact that it was taken by someone of our order."

Catherine had no answer. Fear was burrowing into her heart.

"Mother," she asked. "Sister Genevieve wasn't well yesterday, a bad cough. Did she attend Vespers?"

"No, she asked to be allowed to rest, and with all the guests we thought the coughing would be . . . Oh, Catherine!" Her face froze. "It can't be. Her own brother!"

"And she has my baby!"

Catherine raced to the cloister garden, where she found Margaret alone with Edana. Setting James down, she clutched the child to her in relief. Then she asked where Sister Genevieve had gone.

"She left a few moments ago," Margaret told them. "She said she had something to clean up."

"Where?" Catherine asked sharply.

Margaret pointed toward the woods.

Catherine gave Edana back and ran for Abbess Heloise.

"She's gone toward the river!"

Both women hurried in that direction, Heloise stopping only to send one of the lay brothers to fetch Lord Milo and Count Thibault to follow them.

They found Genevieve up to her knees in the water, trying to push a bundle down among the reeds.

"Sister!" Heloise cried. "My dear, whatever are you doing? You're ill; you'll catch your death in that cold water!"

Genevieve looked up in panic, but didn't move.

Behind them, Lord Milo came running up. When he saw what was happening, all the color drained from his face.

"Genevieve!" he shouted. "Oh, no, not again!"

Heloise spun to face him, hers eyes blazing.

"What do you mean 'again'?" she demanded.

Milo jerked back from her anger. "She always had an odd streak, but she's never killed anyone before!" he protested.

Heloise grew icily calm. "But she did other things? She was unbalanced when she came to us and not one of her family bothered to tell us?"

Milo looked over the abbess' shoulder to where Genevieve had returned to her task, oblivious to the gathering crowd.

"We thought that the calm of the cloister would heal her spirit," Milo said. "She was eager to come. Only Roric opposed it. He believed we should keep her under guard at home. But we convinced him it was best for her to be put away here."

"Put away!" Heloise was livid. "Milo, this is a convent, not a prison! We can't care for a madwoman."

While they debated, Catherine was trying to reach Genevieve. She waded into the water, speaking softly as she came.

"Let me help you." She tried to smile. "I'm sorry about the charter yesterday. You were right. Here, I see your problem. The axe is tangled in your robes. If I take it, you can get the bundle free of the reeds."

Genevieve stared at her, then down at the axe handle, sticking out from the mass of stained cloth.

"You gave him a drink of your medicine, didn't you?" Catherine tried to keep her voice soothing. "Sister Melisende told you the dosage to bring about sleep. It still must have been hard for you to cut him up."

"Oh, no." Genevieve looked at her with pride. "At home I used to practice on deer and sheep."

Catherine shivered, forcing her breath to remain steady. She had to reach the axe.

"But how did you get him into the cask?" she asked. "You must be very strong."

"Oh, yes. After I cut him up, I still had to empty many buckets of wine to make room for him." Genevieve stopped to show Catherine her muscular arm. "I said the psalms as I went so I'd know the time. Then I wrapped him up in his clothes and put him bit by bit in the cask. But he wouldn't sink, so I had to use the laundry paddle."

She spoke as if the explanation was clear, returning to her task with an expression of determination.

"But, why, Genevieve? Did your brother hurt you?" Slowly Catherine reached for the axe.

The nun seemed bewildered. She had finally noticed the men on the bank just behind Catherine: her uncle, brothers, the count and his son.

"I loved him so I had to save him," she told them all. "He spent his life in mortal sin. I had to immerse him in the Blood of Christ to make him change his ways. It's too bad that he wouldn't fit in the vat in one piece. But I saved them all so that he'll be resurrected whole."

She grinned at them, waiting for praise.

At that moment, Catherine grabbed the axe and backed quickly away. As she did, Genevieve's family splashed in, took hold of her and led her back to the convent.

Catherine was panting with delayed terror as she handed the axe to a lay brother and leaned weakly against Heloise.

"Mother, please don't ever tell my husband what I just did," she begged.

Heloise patted her shoulder. "I promise never to mention it, but I can't be so certain of Count Thibault. You were very foolish, you know."

Catherine agreed.

Heloise squared her shoulders. "Now I must decide what's to be done with Genevieve. Lord Milo, a word with you!"

Catherine never heard that word, but when Milo set off for the Holy Land, he had less for provisions than he had anticipated and the Paraclete had the resources to see that Genevieve was never left alone again.

Light Her Way Home

Originally, I had planned this to be part of a book, but sometimes things don't fit. I found Petronilla in the charters of Paris, a collection I would recommend to anyone needing a good plot. She came from a wealthy family. Her brother really was a money-changer and she paid her own upkeep from an inheritance so that she could live as an anchoress in what is now the heart of Paris. It was first published in Murder Most Crafty, *edited by Maggie Bruce, published by Berkley in 2005. The theme for this was arts and crafts and I have no talent for either, so I explained how to make lavender scented candles, something I did in college. I didn't render the tallow myself, though. Back then it was paraffin. My explanation is also at the end of the book.*

Paris, Autumn 1150

Edgar of Wedderlie, merchant of Paris, looked up from the silver wire he was trying to thread around a piece of deep golden amber.

"Catherine," he asked his wife, "where are you going with six of our best candles?"

Catherine started. She'd been hoping to leave without him noticing. She stopped with a sigh. He'd find out sooner or later.

"Margaret and I are taking them to St. Lazare," she told him. "As an offering for the prayers of the anchoress."

Edgar shook his head. "One candle is more than her prayers are worth," he said. "Everyone knows that the woman spends more time gossiping at her window than on her knees."

"Edgar, that's not true!" Catherine answered with indignation. "Petronilla can't help it if so many people come to her for prayers and advice. She spends much of the night reading her Psalter and asking Our Lady to help us. That's why she should have good candles."

Edgar knew he would lose this one, but he wanted one more sally. "And just why do we need help?" He grinned to show he was now teasing. "Don't I keep us all fed and housed? And won't you soon have a lovely new amber necklace?"

Catherine nodded, "You take good care of us," she assured him. "But this is not the only world. This is for *your* soul," she counted off the candles. "This for Margaret; three for the children and this one," she gave it a caress, "is for the soul of our poor Heloisa."

The mention of the baby that had died ended the pretense of argument. Edgar turned his face back to his work, his pale hair hiding his expression.

"Be back by dark," he said. "And make sure my sister remembers to wear her warm scarf."

It was only after she left that he realized that she had not taken a candle for prayers for herself. He shook his head. They could have spared one more.

Catherine and Edgar's sister Margaret hurried through the streets up to the abbey of St. Lazare. It was late autumn and the black mud of Paris stuck to their wooden *sabots*, so that each step made a sucking noise. The hems of their robes were soon heavy with it. Around them, other women had tied up their skirts between their legs to be able to move more easily. Catherine wished she had done the same before they left the house.

The two women made their way to the edge of the city, where the monks had built a hospital as a refuge to care for lepers. There seemed to be more of them since King Louis had taken so many knights and soldiers to fight in the Holy Land. Of those who returned from the east, there were few who had escaped some illness or injury. The lepers were the saddest.

It was against the chapel wall of this hospital that the anchoress Petronilla had chosen to build her cell. It was only a frame and plaster building of one chamber. A slit in the back wall allowed her to see into the church, participate in the mass and receive the Host. A small window on the other side was to allow her communication with the world.

Each day food and other provisions were delivered and the waste bucket taken out and emptied.

Catherine felt it a slander to say that the anchoress spent all her time in gossip. On the contrary, Petronilla kept her own counsel better than many priests. People came to her to unburden their hearts and souls of their troubles. They asked her for prayers and advice. Pilgrims came from miles away to speak with her. It was said that Petronilla had the gift of solace. Many left her with grateful tears. What deep secrets Petronilla had been told, she never revealed.

As they neared St. Lazare, Catherine and Margaret noticed that even in the autumn rain, there were a few supplicants waiting to speak with Petronilla.

"Perhaps we should just leave the candles with the porter," Catherine suggested. "He'll have her confessor deliver them along with our message."

"I don't mind waiting," Margaret said. "I'd like to speak with her."

Catherine gave Margaret a worried glance. What did a girl of seventeen have to confess?

"Are you thinking of retreating from the world?" she asked, keeping her voice light.

Margaret laughed. "If I were, I'd go back to the convent, not build a hermitage at a crossroad."

But something had been troubling Margaret ever since she had returned home at the end of summer. Catherine suspected the cause but was too afraid of the answer to question her. Perhaps Petronilla could give Margaret wiser guidance than the family was able to.

When their turn came, Catherine hoped that Margaret wouldn't be too long. She was shocked at how wan the anchoress looked.

"God save you," the woman greeted them.

"And you, blessed sister," Catherine answered. "Forgive me, but are you well?"

Petronilla smiled. "I am a bit tired, nothing more."

She glanced over Catherine's shoulder. Catherine turned to see the man who had been there before them trudging disconsolately away. Catherine turned back to Petronilla, who sighed,

"My confessor warns me not to exceed my strength but I know that God will give me what I need to continue," she said.

"Of course." Catherine took the candles out of her basket. "We made these from the best beeswax and scented them with lavender to soothe the spirit. May they be of some use to you."

"You are very kind." Petronilla accepted the gift. "I shall pray for you and your family. I admit that it is easier to concentrate on the psalms with the odor of lavender and honey in my nostrils rather than the meaty smell of tallow candles."

She sighed. "If I were truly as devout as people believe, I could make my devotions in the middle of a slaughterhouse and not notice."

"But there is no need for that," Catherine said. "You are afflicted enough with visitors to test your steadfastness."

"You are not an affliction, Catherine," Petronilla assured her. "And even the most worrisome of those who come to me remind me of how fortunate I am to be able to remain in my cell rather than face a daily struggle just to survive."

"Ah, that's it," Catherine thought. *"She is weary from the cares of others, not her own."*

Margaret must have felt this as well, for she didn't ask for a private moment with Petronilla as planned. Or it may have been because of the rain, now turning to sleet. Catherine was relieved that they could leave, for her felt hat was sodden. Water dripped from the brim into her scarf and down her cheeks. Warm wool helped but the chill found its way in.

Twilight was settling in as they left. Catherine was fretting about the rain and the chances of getting back before darkness made the twisting streets unrecognizable. She didn't see the figure waiting to speak to the anchoress, but Margaret noticed in time to pull Catherine aside before they collided.

"Who was that?" she asked as they slipped and slid back to the house.

"A man, I think," Margaret answered. "There was a sharp smell to him. I could have sworn it was the same one who was there when we arrived. Did you notice?"

"No, nothing but the rain running down my neck," Catherine said. "Oh, my hands are freezing!"

As soon as they entered the house, they threw off their damp woolen cloaks, slipped out of the rough wooden shoes and hurried to the hearth. The dying light had stopped Edgar's work and he was waiting for them impatiently.

"Have the children been fed?" Catherine asked as he handed her a bowl of egg and cabbage soup.

"Long ago," he answered. "They're upstairs with Martin, probably destroying something."

Catherine nodded. She knew her children.

Margaret gave her brother a kiss. "Don't scold us, Edgar. We had to wait to see the anchoress."

Edgar poured a cup of wine and gave it to her, then filled his own.

"I don't understand why this woman draws so many to her," Edgar complained. "I've heard about her at the merchants' meetings. She's the daughter of a money-changer. Her brother keeps the changing window on the *Grand Pont*. I bring my coins to him to weigh. That's not exactly a spiritual beginning."

Catherine shrugged. "Who knows why God chooses some for a contemplative life? I go to her because . . ." She paused. "Now that I think of it, I don't know why. Petronilla gives me a sense of peace. There is an air about her. She listens, smiles and nods, promises to pray for me, and I go home feeling better. That sounds rather silly, doesn't it?"

Margaret had been silent up until then, warming her face and feet at the fire. Now she spoke up.

"I don't think so," she stated. "She makes me feel that way, too. I don't care that she comes from money-changers. When we talk, my problems seem easier to bear."

"Well, then," Edgar closed the conversation. "That alone is worth the cost of the candles."

Winter closed in early that year. The earthen streets of Paris were crisscrossed with wooden slats to keep carts from sinking into the mud. But these were soon slick with icy rain so that, even in solid wooden *sabots*, people slid from one end of the town to the other, grateful if they did not break a parcel or a limb in the process.

Catherine and her family stayed in much of the time. With three small children and a large dog in the house, she often thought wistfully of Petronilla's solitary cell.

Without warning, there came a clear day. The sun shone warmly, drying the streets. Everyone hurried out to the market for supplies and gossip.

The crowd was thick around the honey and wax stall, voices high with distress. Catherine stopped at the edge to learn what was causing the commotion.

"Dreadful! Just dreadful!" Josta the ribbon seller was wiping her eyes. "The poor dear saint!"

"Catherine!" Her neighbor, Hervig, caught at her arm. "Have you heard? There was a fire last night at St. Lazare. Petronilla is dead!"

"What? A fire? But how?" The horror of being trapped in a doorless cell hit her all at once. Catherine felt short of breath.

"No one knows," Hervig said. "Perhaps a lamp spilled or a candle came too near the curtain."

"There's a corner of the roof all burned away," Josta added. "And one wall is down. They say a man coming home from a tavern saw the flames and tore down the plaster walls to pull her out but it was too late."

"Her body is lying in the chapel," someone volunteered. "I'm going to pray before it as soon as the shopping's done. I've no doubt someone will receive a miracle even before she's buried."

Catherine didn't participate in the discussion of Petronilla's almost certain sainthood. She was overwhelmed by the tragic circumstances of her death.

Margaret had been several steps behind Catherine, struggling to keep the two oldest children, James and Edana, from wandering off. She arrived just in time to hear someone announce, "They say her hands are scraped bloody from trying to claw her way out of the room. Poor Petronilla! How awful to be burned to death!"

"Petronilla! No! It can't be." The last sentence was hardly more than a whisper. Margaret's hands slipped from those of the children as she struggled to remain upright.

"Margaret!" Catherine dropped her vegetable basket as she reached out to catch her sister-in-law. "James, take your sister; run straight home and get Papa." She rounded on the crowd. "Where is your respect? We should be on our knees instead of standing about telling stories of such horror."

In Catherine's arms, Margaret gave a gasp and then began crying so piteously that many of those around felt ashamed.

"My dear." Catherine hugged her. "It's dreadful, I know, but you mustn't take this so much to heart. I'm sure Petronilla is now in Heaven."

Margaret wiped her eyes on her sleeve. "Please, take me home," she begged.

Everyone stared as the two women made their way across the market square. But they immediately returned to their business as Edgar came running toward them. He was known in the city as a man not to cross even if he had only one hand.

They got Margaret home and to bed. As they came back down into the hall Edgar looked a question at Catherine.

"I don't know why she reacted so strongly," she answered. "I didn't think Margaret knew the anchoress that well. Certainly not enough to be so distraught even at such a sudden death. She's exchanged no more than a few words with Petronilla."

"Can you ask her when she wakes?"

Catherine shook her head. "I'm not sure that would be wise. She's been very reticent since she came home. When I try to find out what's bothering her, she only smiles and denies any worry."

They entered the hall, empty but for the smoldering charcoal brazier that only took the edge off the chill in the room. Edgar poked at the coals, then added a few more from the bucket.

"Perhaps," he spoke slowly, his eyes on the glowing coals. "Perhaps we should join those keeping watch on the body in the church."

Catherine looked at him in surprise. She knew he was worried about his sister. Catherine was, too. Margaret had only two choices, to enter the convent or accept a husband chosen by her powerful grandfather. Neither of these appealed. But Margaret was nearly eighteen, the age when the convent would accept her, and well past the age for marriage. Something had to be decided soon.

Edgar must be more concerned than she thought to grasp at the straw of the chance of a bit of overheard gossip enlightening them.

But she had planned to visit the church in any case, to add her prayers for the soul of the anchoress. "I would welcome your company," she said.

He looked at her and smiled. "A walk alone together with no children hanging from our sleeves? I would enjoy that too, despite the occasion."

They set out later that afternoon, the pale sun still hanging just above the rooftops of the city. It was a long walk to St. Lazare. No one wanted a hospice for lepers in the center of Paris.

The church was ablaze with light and full of people. Monks stood around the body to be sure no one tried to take a piece of clothes or hair or even a finger or two as relics.

Catherine and Edgar shuffled forward, stepping around people lying flat on the stone floor, wailing their sorrow.

To Catherine's relief, Petronilla did not look as though she'd been through a fire. Her short hair had been washed and she'd been placed in a white robe. The only sign of burning was a bright redness around her mouth and across her nose and her torn and bruised hands.

They both crossed themselves and said a prayer for the poor young woman. Then they made their way out to the porch of the church, where several people had already gathered.

"That's the brother, Radulf," Edgar whispered, nodding toward a man in his thirties. He had an air of prosperity and wore a rich fur cloak held closed by a golden brooch.

The man was standing next to a woman whom Catherine assumed to be his wife. Both were weeping, dabbing at their eyes frequently with handkerchiefs. Around them, people patted their shoulders ineffectually.

"Should we speak to him?" she asked Edgar.

"Let's wait a bit and listen," he answered.

Catherine wondered how long they would be able to keep from being pushed out into the road by the flood of people coming and going. She leaned against the wall of the porch and dug in her heels.

Next to her, two men were talking.

"Terrible accident," the younger commented. "God's will is beyond my understanding."

"Well, that's a surprise," his companion said. "Did you get anything?"

"Just a bit of burnt rush from the roof of her cell," the younger complained. "I know those monks. They'll be tighter than mussels with the relics."

The first sighed. "Well, we might get some more of the roof and sell pieces to the pilgrims when they come."

Catherine turned away from them with distaste. The men went on talking.

"Good thing for Radulf, though," the young one said, picking something out of a back tooth. "He gets the changing house and a sainted sister."

"I wonder if he has anything of hers at his house," the other man said. "Maybe we could get some old robes cheap and cut them up to wrap around the charred rushes."

They finally moved off.

"Edgar," Catherine asked, "what did they mean about Petronilla's brother getting the changing house? I thought it was already his."

Edgar rubbed his eyes. The smoke from a hundred candles was slithering out into the porch.

"I think I heard something about that," he answered. "Radulf's father left the building to Petronilla. I don't think he trusted Radulf to take care of her. At least that was the rumor."

"Then he didn't pay for her maintenance in the anchorage?" Catherine was surprised.

"I think she paid her own way from the rent on the changing house," Edgar said. "But it's no affair of ours, Catherine."

"I know," Catherine said doubtfully. "It just seems a strange situation."

"Edgar!"

As they pushed their way out, Edgar had come nose to nose with a man trying to enter the church.

He grimaced. "God save you, Maurice."

"And you," Maurice laughed. "The last person I'd expect to see here."

He glanced at Catherine and smirked. "Ah, now I understand."

Catherine started to giggle. Edgar gave her a sharp nudge.

"I don't believe you've met my wife, have you, Maurice?" he said. "Catherine, Maurice is a trader in leather."

Catherine had guessed that from the faint odor of urine he carried with him. She bowed.

"Oh, of course!" Maurice said. "God save you, *ma dame*." He tried to cover his embarrassment. "My wife sent me to help stand watch. She's ill, or she would have come herself."

"I shall pray for her recovery," Catherine said politely.

"By the way, Edgar," Maurice continued, "I met your sister last night, not far from here. She may have told you that I offered to escort her home."

"You must be mistaken," Edgar answered coldly. "Margaret did not go out last night."

"Edgar, I may not know your wife, but I've seen your sister," Maurice insisted. "That red hair is striking enough, along with the scar across her cheek. If you didn't know she was out then I'm sorry to have to tell you, but I'm sure you wouldn't want to be kept in ignorance."

He didn't appear sorry. Catherine was torn between alarm at his news and a strong desire to strike him. By the tension in his body, she knew that Edgar felt the same.

They left before they could act on their impulse.

"Do you think he really saw Margaret?" Catherine asked. "I was sure she had gone up to bed."

"So was I," Edgar answered shortly.

His anger sizzled in the cold air. Catherine said no more until they reached the house. She put her hand on Edgar's arm as they entered.

"If it's true," she pleaded, "I'm sure there's a good reason."

"Not good enough to put her life in danger," Edgar said.

Margaret was sitting alone by the dying embers of the charcoal brazier. She lifted her head at the sound of their steps.

Edgar was prepared to chastise his sister harshly, but one look at the abject despair in her eyes and his anger melted.

She sighed deeply.

"I was afraid Maurice would speak to you. I would rather have told you myself," she told them quietly. "I had to see Petronilla. She told me that it would be the last time we could speak."

"What do you mean?" Catherine knelt next to her. "Did she prophesy her own death?"

"I don't know; I never saw her. I was going to, but there was someone with her," Margaret told them. "I thought it might be her confessor in the church, but it sounded as though he were right in the cell with her."

"But how?" Edgar asked. "The man who tried to rescue her had to rip out the wall."

"I don't know." Margaret lowered her face. Her voice was barely a whisper. "He was shouting at her. I couldn't hear all the words. As I came close, he yelled, 'You cursed her!' and she cried, 'No, it was your sin that did it!'"

Edgar looked at Catherine. "That doesn't sound like a conversation with her confessor," he said.

Catherine's forehead creased with thought.

"Margaret," she said at last. "We need to talk with you about the reason you felt it so necessary to go out after dark to see Petronilla."

"Yes, I know." Her voice wavered. "But first, Catherine, you must find out who killed her."

The next morning, Catherine and Edgar stood before the remains of the anchorage. There was a hole waist-high in the wall, guarded by a burly lay brother of St. Lazare leaning on a thick staff.

"The abbot has authorized me to strike anyone who tries to enter," he said. "He's been appalled by you relic hunters."

"We want no relics," Edgar said. "Only to look."

The man allowed them to approach but stayed nearby, tapping the staff meaningfully.

The walls inside the cell were streaked black with soot. One corner of the roof had burnt away entirely. The floor was littered with charred bits of fallen rushes. Edgar stared at them for some time.

"Do you think Margaret was right?" Catherine asked him. "It seems impossible. Even if someone wanted her dead, how could they have entered?"

"I know how," Edgar said, still examining the floor of the cell. "How the killer entered and, I think, how she was killed. The real question is why."

"She knew many secrets," Catherine considered. "Someone might have regretted confessing to her. If that's true, I don't see how we'll ever know who, unless they were seen."

"As Margaret was?" Edgar reminded her.

Catherine felt a shiver run down her back. Edgar had thought further ahead than she had. If they announced that Petronilla had been murdered, the first suspect might be Edgar's sister.

"What can we do?" she asked.

Edgar chewed his lip, still staring at the debris inside the cell. Finally, he turned back to Catherine.

"This was a horrible murder, both cruel and sacrilegious," he said. "It is our duty to find the killer and bring him to justice."

Catherine agreed that this would be the best course. She also pointed out that discovering the one who had killed the anchoress and proving it might entail a great deal of work.

"Then we had better start now," Edgar said. "First, I want to examine the body more closely."

"Good luck with that! The monks won't let you near her," Catherine reminded him.

"I know; that's why you'll have to do it. I'll tell you what to look for."

They went around the hospital to the church and found that the crowds had thinned as the day waned. In a few moments they were standing in front of the mortal remains of Petronilla.

"Please let me through," she begged the guard. "I only want to kiss her good-bye."

"And snip a bit of her robe or a bit of her skin." He moved to block her way.

"Only a kiss and a blessing," Catherine promised. "She was my friend."

The guard made the mistake of looking directly into her eyes. They were startlingly blue against her olive skin and sparkling with tears.

"Very well," he said. "Keep your hands behind your back and be quick."

Catherine did as told. As she bent over the body, Catherine murmured a prayer and then kissed the bright red cheek, inhaling deeply as she did so.

"Thank you," she told the guard, giving him a coin. "For the poor."

By the time they got outside, she was shaking.

"You were right," she told Edgar.

He nodded grimly. "I think that the first thing in the morning, we need to pay a visit of condolence on Petronilla's brother."

Radulf the money-changer was at his window on the bridge soon after dawn the next day. He forced a smile as Edgar and Catherine approached.

"Lord Edgar, my Lady, God save you," he greeted them. "Brought me more coins from foreign parts?"

"Only some *sous* from Rouen and Toulouse." Edgar handed him a small bag. "I don't like the look of the Norman ones. I fear they're light weight."

Radulf shook his head. "It's a sorry world," he said with feeling.

He took out a metal dish to put the coins in. "The silver seems good, if a bit light." He balanced them in his palm, a dozen pieces, each no bigger than a fingernail. His hand shook.

Catherine gave a sympathetic sigh.

"The death of your sister must grieve you terribly," she said. "We plan on attending the funeral Mass tomorrow."

"It's kind of you," he said. "Petronilla and I didn't always agree, but I shall miss her. Still, I hope you're not one of those who insist that she's a saint."

"Well," Catherine wasn't certain how she should respond. "Petronilla was a pious woman who gave her life to God . . ." she began.

"And died for that. Nevertheless, those monks will ensure she has a shrine and a few miracles by spring," Radulf continued. "Now that she's left them this house."

"She gave your home to St. Lazare?" Edgar asked in surprise.

"For our sins, she said," he told them sourly. "She might have asked if I wanted my sins forgiven and no place to work. The prior was here yesterday to tell me they're doubling my rent."

He finished testing the coins and gave Edgar their equivalent in money of Paris.

"I'm looking for a place near the road to St. Denis," he told them. "I hope you'll come find me."

"It seems he had every reason to keep his sister alive," Catherine said as they walked back toward their home.

"I was afraid it wouldn't be so simple," Edgar agreed. "You don't think someone from St. Lazare could have . . ."

Catherine was horrified at the idea but forced herself to examine it.

"Murder for the sake of the rent on a building?" she said. "It's not as if the hospital is poor."

"What about murder for the alms that they will now receive in memory of the saint?" Edgar asked. "And the increased numbers of pilgrims."

"That would be a stronger reason," Catherine admitted. "But I can't help but think that the monks would be more subtle."

They had reached the house. Edgar stopped at the gate.

"What should we tell my sister?" he asked.

"Everything we know," Catherine took his hand. "Maybe she can help."

They called Margaret in at once.

"You weren't mistaken," Edgar told her. "There was someone in the cell with Petronilla just before she died."

"Are you sure?" Margaret asked.

"The roof was burnt entirely through at one corner," Catherine explained. "But the hole was made before the fire. The thatch on the floor was still whole."

Margaret nodded. "Mother Heloise always told us that a convent, or an anchorage, were kept unharmed more by the power of belief than stout walls. Someone hated her more than they feared God."

"Or feared her," Edgar said. "I think whoever it was wanted her to keep silence. Perhaps he tried to frighten her."

He paused and turned to Catherine. "Shall I tell her?"

"Of course," Catherine answered.

Edgar took a deep breath. "Petronilla had burns on her face, but they were light, in a ring around her mouth and over her nose. You'd think the monks would have wondered."

"When I bent to kiss her, I saw a sheen of wax at the edge of the burn," Catherine added. "And there was the scent of lavender."

Margaret's eyes grew wide with horror. "He used our candles!"

"I didn't find her cooking pot," Edgar said. "I think he dropped a candle into it, held her down and poured the melted wax over her nose and down her throat. She didn't burn; she was smothered."

Margaret closed her eyes and moaned. Suddenly, her head jerked up.

"It was on his hand," she said. "The leather seller. When he caught up with me and offered to take me home. He gave me his hand and it smelled of lavender. I thought he used scent to cover the stink of his occupation."

"Maurice? But what reason could he have had?" Edgar found it hard to believe. "Did he even know her?"

"Yes," Catherine said. "He was there when we brought the candles. Margaret remarked on the smell of his clothes then. And why else would he have been at St. Lazare that night? He probably saw Margaret from the window and chased after her."

"He must have killed her right after I started home," Margaret shuddered. "The voices stopped while I was trying to decide what to do. I must have made a noise."

Edgar and Catherine both embraced Margaret, each realizing how close she had come to being the second victim. But Margaret was still preoccupied with the cold-bloodedness of Maurice's actions.

"And after he decided I hadn't seen him," she went on, "he returned to set the fire. If someone else hadn't come by and pulled her out, no one would have known how she died."

Edgar reached for his cloak.

"Where are you going?" Catherine asked in alarm.

"To the provost," he said.

"But we still don't know why Maurice killed her," she said.

"I think it has to do with his wife's illness," he said. "How long has it been since anyone has seen her? Didn't Maurice travel with the king to the Holy Land?"

"You think he brought back a disease?" Catherine knew there were other things beside leprosy that were also caught through sin. "And his wife told Petronilla?"

"The king's men will find out," he told her. "Whatever sin he was trying to hide, he has committed a greater one. I am more concerned to see him captured before he realizes that we know what he did."

Catherine had one more worry. "Before you go, Edgar. Margaret, can you tell us what you needed to talk to Petronilla about?"

Margaret sighed. "I had nothing to confess, if you were fearful. I only wanted her to help me to face what I know I must do. I have no calling to be a nun. I wish I did. Therefore, I am going to tell my grandfather that I will marry whomever he chooses for me."

"Oh, my dear!" Catherine said. "There must be something else you can do."

Margaret smiled sadly. "No, there isn't. You both know that. But Grandfather has promised not to make me go too far from those I love. Petronilla made me see that duty need not be sacrifice. I shall miss her."

As Edgar went out to inform the provost of Maurice's crime, he reflected that nothing the man might have done could be worse than depriving the world of a woman of such wisdom.

Catherine and the Sibyl

I decided to give Margaret one more chance at life in the convent. I really didn't want her married. So Catherine and Edgar decided to see if she would be happy at the new monastic house that a brilliant woman named Hildegarde was establishing in the German town of Rupertsberg near Bingen. It was fun to learn more about building techniques, something Edgar was always fascinated by. This comes from The Mammoth Book of Historical Whodunnits *Vol. III, edited by Mike Ashley and published by Robinson, London. 2005*

Rupertsberg, Germany, October, 1151

The day was clear and cloudless, a rare gift in late autumn. Albrecht was eager to get back to work on the church for the new convent. Unlike many of the other workers, he had no fear of climbing on the skeletal scaffolds set up along the walls. He loved looking out across the river Nahe to the valley beyond. He imagined sometimes that he could see his village, where his wife and children waited for him to return in the spring.

He climbed the scaffolding with confidence. He had faith in his skill at carpentry and that of the master builder. Even more, he had faith in the visions of the prioress. Many, including the pope, admitted that God spoke to her directly. If she said they should erect the buildings at this site, so close to the river, then it was certain that it was according to a heavenly plan.

Albrecht swung across the beams of the roof, landing on the platform suspended from the far wall.

There was a loud crack as the narrow board split, sending Albrecht tumbling to the stone floor.

His last emotion was astonishment. God's plan should not have included someone working by night with a saw to slice the board almost through.

In his palace in the city of Troyes, Thibault, count of Champagne, glared at his granddaughter. He was trying to be patient, but his bad hip was sending knives down his leg and she was being extremely trying.

Margaret opened her eyes wide in an effort to keep tears from spilling over. She fought a nervous urge to chew the end of her red braid.

"You are eighteen years old, girl," Thibault barked. "I've offered to find you a suitable husband or dower you enough to enter any convent you wished. Why can't you make up your mind?"

From a corner in the shadows, Catherine watched this trial of her husband's sister. She longed to interrupt but knew this was not the time or place. And what could she say? Tolerant though he usually was, Thibault would not be pleased to learn that his Margaret had long ago decided upon the impossible. She had fallen in love with a Jew.

Catherine sighed. She had thought this folly merely a child's fondness, but as she grew older, Margaret's attachment to Solomon had only deepened and now Catherine feared Solomon returned the feeling. Keeping them apart had no effect. Something irrevocable had to be done.

Margaret knew that to admit her feelings could mean death for Solomon and shame for herself. She had stalled as long as she could. She closed her eyes and let the tears flow where they would. But when she spoke, her voice was steady.

"My lord," she bowed her head and quickly wiped her cheeks with her sleeve. "You have been more than indulgent with my indecision. I beg your forgiveness. I have thought long upon this for I seem to have a vocation for neither monasticism nor marriage."

"Well, those are your choices, Margaret," Thibault said. "You can hardly set up as a seller of trinkets in the market square."

Since that was close to what she did want, Margaret bit her tongue before she spoke again.

"Therefore, rather then inflict myself upon a man who deserves a devoted wife, I shall become a bride of Christ and pray that He send me the grace to be worthy of Him."

Thibault nearly cheered. "Splendid! I'll have Countess Mahaut make arrangements for you to enter the Paraclete. Don't weep, child. It's close enough that your family can visit you often."

"No!" Margaret took a step closer to him. "I love the Paraclete, but I cannot stay there. I must go somewhere else, somewhere far away."

"What?" Catherine leapt to her feet, knocking over the stool she had been sitting on. "You can't do that! Please, my lord Count, don't let her leave us."

The count gave her a look that reminded her she was only in the room on sufferance. Margaret's choice was not in her power to change.

Thibault rose from his chair and put his arms around Margaret.

"I had thought to make the break a gentler one by letting you stay nearby," he said. "But I agree that it might be easier for you to start your new life in new surroundings. Now, have you considered where you wish to go?"

Margaret avoided looking at Catherine as she answered.

"Yes, I want to join the sisters at the new convent at Rupertsberg."

Thibault released her quickly. "The one that the visionary woman is building? I don't know. The pope and Abbot Bernard seem to think well of her, but I understand she can be very difficult."

Margaret didn't answer. Thibault thought another minute.

"Still, she only accepts women from the best families," he considered. "It might be even better than a marriage alliance. And, of course," he added hastily, "Hildegarde has a great reputation for wisdom and piety as well. Yes, it might be the best place for you. I'll see to it."

"Thank you, Grandfather," Margaret whispered.

She left the room.

Catherine looked at the count in stupefaction. He shrugged.

"You heard for yourself," he told her. "Margaret made her choice. Can you and your husband accompany her there?"

Numbly, Catherine nodded.

At Rupertsberg, Albrecht was buried quietly. Prioress Hildegarde promised his widow that she and the children would be cared for and saw to it that his name was added to the book of the dead for whom the nuns prayed.

"A terrible accident," she said to Ludwig, the master builder. "I thought the men always went up in pairs."

She looked at him with an intensity that seemed to stake him to the ground.

"They should," the Master answered. "Albrecht always was one for climbing on his own, though. He used to laugh at the men who didn't like being up so high."

The prioress shook her head. "He should not have had to pay such a price for his hubris."

"No, my lady." Ludwig wasn't sure what hubris was, but could agree it was not a sin worth dying for. He hoped he would soon be dismissed. There were things that worried him about Albrecht's 'accident' and he would rather the Lady Hildegarde didn't find out about them. He bowed. Perhaps she would take the hint and let him leave.

"Ludwig?"

He looked up. Hildegarde was gazing over his head at the church. With a heart full of dread, Ludwig turned around.

He saw nothing amiss. The walls of an earlier church were being cannibalized to build the one for the nuns. Chunks of old stone blocks stuck with cement lay in a pile next to the rising nave of the new building. The men were working. Embrich was dutifully walking the treadmill that helped the scaffolding to rise. Ludwig hoped he wouldn't take a swig from his beerskin while the prioress was watching. The man was the worst worker he had ever hired. The treadmill was the only task he could be trusted to do properly.

He turned back to Hildegarde, still wary. Everyone knew she was a prophet, the only one in the modern world. Perhaps she saw disaster in their future.

"Yes, my lady," he quavered.

"This isn't the first accident we have had," she said, still looking, for all Ludwig knew, into the soul of the earth, demanding answers from Nature herself.

"No, my lady," he admitted. "There was the problem with the cracked windlass, and some rope has gone missing, but these things happen in all projects."

"Do they?" The prioress' expression told him that he had better to see to it that nothing more happened on this one.

Margaret's brother Edgar had not been pleased with her decision to enter Hildegarde's convent. But there was little he could do in the face of the count's approval.

"They've only been building it for a year or so," he grumbled. "How do we even know she'll have a roof over her head?"

"If you're not certain about the place, we could stop at Trier for a few days on the way there, to visit my sister," Catherine suggested to him. "If there is anything irregular about the convent, Agnes will know."

"Do you think we could leave the children with her while we go on to Rupertsberg?" Edgar asked hopefully.

"It would be good for her to have them," Catherine agreed.

The promise of time alone with his wife eased somewhat the prospect of leaving his much-loved little sister with foreign nuns.

But not completely.

"I don't see why she has to marry or enter a convent," he grumbled. "I can provide for her here."

"You and Solomon are partners," Catherine reminded him. "You would both provide for her."

Edgar gave her a sharp glance. Solomon was his best friend, but . . .

"If we're to reach Germany before winter," he decided, "we'll have to leave at once. I doubt Solomon will be back from Rome before we go. Margaret will have to leave him a letter."

Sadly, Catherine agreed. It bothered her greatly that Margaret was entering the religious life because she couldn't marry the man she loved. But better to find a haven as the bride of Christ than suffer the danger and shame of abandoning her faith for a Jew, no matter how good a man he might be.

Catherine's sister Agnes had married into a good German family near the city of Trier. Her husband was the uncle of the present lord, Peter, a young man of twenty. Until he married, Agnes was happy to run the household. Peter suspected that she would continue to do so even after that happened. He hoped his unknown wife wouldn't mind.

"Of course I know about Hildegarde," she told Catherine, Edgar and Margaret over dinner on the night they arrived. "You must remember how they read the account of her visions at that council here in Trier. Since Bernard of Clairvaux and the pope agreed that they were genuine, almost everyone has been asking her to tell their future. And she writes to those who haven't asked, to warn them to mend their wicked ways."

"Her convent doesn't sound exactly like a calm haven," Catherine said with a worried glance at Margaret.

"Hardly." Agnes signaled the servants to clear the cloth and bring in the fruit and sugared almonds. "She's usually in a middle of a whirlwind. At the moment she's decided to move her convent to Rupertsberg. Several of the nuns have rebelled at being dragged from the comfort of St. Disibod and the monks there are furious that she wants to leave their protection, taking her fame and property with her."

"I know these things," Margaret assured them. "I would like to be a part of a new religious foundation. And it would be interesting to have a prophet for an abbess."

"Prioress," Agnes corrected. "She can't get the monks of St. Disibod to free her entirely from their control."

"At least in principle," her husband Meinhard added. "She has her ways. When she had a vision telling her to move to Rupertsberg, they refused to let her go. Remember?"

"Oh, yes," Agnes said. "Then Hildegarde was struck down with a paralyzing illness. The abbot thought she was feigning until he tried to lift her from her bed."

"He said it was as if she were being held in place by a powerful force," Meinhard concluded. "He couldn't move her. Not until he agreed to let her leave."

"You see?" Margaret said. "She is under divine protection. I shall be quite safe there."

Her brother wasn't so sure. "God has a way of protecting his chosen ones right up to the point of martyrdom," he said. "It sounds to me as if you are entering a maelstrom rather than a convent."

"Perhaps I should accompany you there," Peter spoke up. "In case there are problems."

Everyone stared at him. Peter rarely gave an opinion and he had never shown an interest in leaving his own lands.

"You are foreigners and your German, while good, isn't perfect," he explained. "It would be terrible if the kin of my Aunt Agnes came to grief because I wasn't there to speak for them."

Meinhard and Edgar exchanged a long look, then they both turned to consider Margaret, animated with wine. She did not look at all like a nun.

"I believe Peter is right," Edgar said. "We would be pleased to have your company."

Ludwig stood once more before Prioress Hildegarde, twisting his knit cap in his hands.

"The stand for the pitch cauldron was steady," he insisted. "I checked it myself. There was no reason for it to tip over."

Hildegarde nodded. "No natural reason," she agreed.

"My lady!" Ludwig dropped his hat in astonishment. "You don't think there are demons at work in this holy place?"

"The holier the place, the more likely the Evil One is to send his minions to destroy it," Hildegarde said calmly. "Demons are unnecessary, though, when there are enough weak human souls to consent to his desires."

Ludwig gave a deep sigh of relief. He was used to evil in human form. It was monsters from the depths of Hell that frightened him.

"Someone is trying to keep us from finishing the church?" he guessed. "Who would be so foolhardy? You would know them at once, wouldn't you?"

The prioress smiled gently. "I am but the servant of the Living Light," she explained. "I do not ask for revelation, but accept it when it comes to me. We shall have to find the miscreant ourselves. Of course, it's possible that a vision may be sent while we are endeavoring to do so."

She seemed so confident that Ludwig felt ashamed of the worry still gnawing at his gut. He bowed and backed to the door.

"Ludwig!"

He froze to the spot. Had God spoken to the lady while he was still in the room?

"Ludwig," she repeated. "You forgot your hat."

That afternoon, Hildegarde called one of the nuns into her chamber.

"Richardis," she greeted the woman with a tender smile. "How are my daughters doing in their new home?"

"Most are offering up the increased discomforts as a sacrifice to Our Lord," Richardis told her. "A few still looked pained. Trauchte's father, Lord Gerlac, is in Bingen, ready to take her to a less austere convent the moment she sends word. She thinks no one knows, but he's been seen lurking outside the dorter walls."

"Has he, now?" Hildegarde did not seem surprised by the knowledge. "I shall remember him in my prayers. Now, I have received a message that the granddaughter of the count of Champagne has requested a visit with the intention of joining our sisterhood. She has apparently been raised at the Paraclete."

Richardis' eyebrows rose. "And she wishes to join us? If it isn't to flee some offense committed there, then she would be a most welcome addition. Heloise's nuns are renowned for their learning."

"I would rather she were renowned for her piety," Hildegarde remarked. "However, both can be ascertained when she and her family arrive. I have had a message from a relative of theirs in Trier. They should be here within a day or so. I only wish that I could find out who has been creating these 'accidents' among the workers before then."

Richardis hesitated. "Relatives in Trier? Mother Hildegarde, I believe I have heard of this Margaret and her family. If you permit it, they might be able to assist us."

Hildegarde was doubtful at first, but as Richardis related what she knew, the prioress began to form a plan.

Catherine had resigned herself to being assigned a bed in the women's section of the guest house. Marital relations were unseemly when one was the guest of celibates. She wasn't prepared though, for how primitive the accommodations were.

"I had heard that *Magistra* Hildegarde encouraged moderation in the renunciation of the flesh," she moaned as she inspected the bare room. "Perhaps her opinion has changed. It's good that we brought our own mattresses. I didn't know we'd need to bring bed frames too."

"I wonder what the conditions are in the nuns' quarters," Margaret said.

"You and I will inspect them thoroughly before I agree to leave you here," Catherine assured her.

"It doesn't matter," Margaret answered. "I am prepared to subjugate my body to the needs of my soul."

Catherine bit her tongue to keep from arguing. Her mind said that Margaret was right, but her heart believed otherwise. Like Edgar, she wished there were a way to keep his sister with them forever.

Edgar hadn't noticed the state of the guest rooms. He had taken one look at the construction work, thrown his pack on the ground and gone to survey the building.

Lugwig growled as he saw Edgar.

"Look sharp, if you can, Embrich," he said to the worker. "We're about to have another visit from some noble know-it-all who wants to give us advice on how to do our jobs, even if he can't tell his axe from his adze."

He turned around to see if Embrich were looking halfway competent and discovered that, wisely, the man had made himself scarce. Ludwig forced a smile.

"Greetings, my lord," he bowed. "Come to see where your daughter will be saying her prayers?"

"Hmm?" Edgar was gazing up at the tower with a worried frown. "Oh, yes. My sister. Building rather close to the edge, aren't you? A few bad winters and the river could eat away your foundations."

This was what Ludwig had thought when the Lady Hildgarde had told him the site, but he'd never admit it to a stranger.

"The rock is solid under the church," he insisted. "We had a hell of a time digging into it."

"That's good," Edgar squinted at something hanging halfway up the tower. "What is that rope attached to?"

Ludwig turned. "It's wrapped around the crank for pulling the baskets of *rubbez* to fill in the space between the walls."

"I see," Edgar smiled. "Why is it hanging from a wooden tower?"

"Trade secret," Ludwig smiled back. "If you'll excuse me, my lord."

He turned and hurried away without waiting for leave. Edgar studied the building for a minute more. A movement by the pile of stones caught his eye. Curious, he wandered over to find a young man dozing against the rubble. As he approached, the man woke with a start. Seeing Edgar, he crossed himself in relief.

"Thank the Virgin!" he exclaimed. "I thought you were Ludwig!"

Edgar smiled at him, noting the bruised hands and dusty clothes.

"Not been at the craft long?" he asked.

A look of fear crossed the man's face. "I'm a journeyman! Don't believe what Master Ludwig says! He has some grudge against me, I don't know why. I didn't slit the canvas on the tents or spill the lime, but I'm the first one he shouts at. Don't tell him, my lord, that you found me asleep. I beg you."

Edgar reassured the man. The tolling of a bell reminded him that Catherine and Margaret were waiting for him.

Catherine met him at the door of the guest house.

"Margaret and I have been speaking with one of the nuns here," she told him. "Prioress Hildegarde has made a very odd request. It seems that there have been a number of unusual problems in the construction of the convent buildings. She thinks she has discovered who is responsible, but needs help in proving it."

Edgar listened.

"What do you think?" Catherine asked when she had finished.

"I think that, whether or not her visions come from Heaven, *Magistra* Hildegarde is a very wise woman," he answered. "Tell her that we will do as she requests."

The next morning Catherine suggested that Peter might like to take Margaret on a short walk around the convent walls.

He agreed with delight.

"Margaret," Catherine whispered as they left. "Remember what I told you."

"I won't do anything foolish," she promised.

As soon as they left, Catherine shook out her skirts and checked the soles of her shoes. "Ready?" she asked Edgar.

"Yes, just don't be too convincing," Edgar kissed her cheek. "I wonder who told Hildegarde that you were inclined to be clumsy."

The clapper was sounding for Sext as Edgar and Catherine headed over to the church. They could hear the chanting of the nuns in their private chapel.

As they drew near, Edgar pointed up at the men working on the scaffolding. Embrich had been promoted to hod carrier. He was carefully climbing a ladder, balancing the box of bricks against his shoulder.

"You see," he told her loudly. "That hod is way over-loaded. No wonder they have so many accidents here. You there! Come down before you lose your grip and fall!"

Startled, Embrich swayed on the ladder, the bricks teetering wildly. Every eye was on him. Suddenly, Catherine gave a cry and tumbled into a pile of hide-covered tools. They clattered to the ground.

"Oh, oh, OW!" she cried, rocking back and forth. "My ankle!"

"What idiot stacked that?" Edger shouted. "You've broken my wife's ankle! Dearest, can you hobble? Who's responsible for this?"

His ranting grew louder until the portress came running from the chapel to see what the problem was.

"I'm not leaving my sister in a place so obviously badly maintained!" Edgar shouted. "My wife may be crippled because of the slovenly behavior of your workmen! What does Lady Hildegarde intend to do about it?"

"My lord, I . . . I have no idea!" The portress stepped away from him. "I shall report this as soon as they are finished saying the Office."

"I want this addressed immediately!" Edgar thundered. "You!" He jabbed his finger at a group of men gaping at him. "Can you be trusted to carry my wife back to the guest house without breaking anything else?"

Catherine had been moaning under his diatribe, rather like a crumhorn accompanying a minstrel's tale. She rocked back and forth in pain but managed to smile weakly as the two men made a cradle of their arms to lift her.

Soon after, the still bewildered workmen were lined up before the church facing Edgar and, even worse, the Lady Hildegarde.

She spoke quietly but even those in the back heard every word.

"I see the dark wind of the North bringing the seeds of evil, destroying our green sanctuary." Hildegarde looked at them sadly then closed her eyes. "I see the Wicked One, like a burrowing vole, finding the weakness in someone's heart and driving him to heed the advice of the serpent."

She opened her eyes and regarded the group of gaping workers.

"I have long been concerned by the number of mishaps involved in the work on my church. The death of Albrecht was not by chance, but design. You all know that one of the boards was tampered with. I tried to convince myself that it was only a jest gone horribly wrong, but too much else has occurred since then. Now this poor woman has also been harmed by the malice at work here. I cannot tolerate it any longer."

Ludwig stepped forward. "I understand, my lady," he said. "I, too, have had my suspicions. I never should have taken on a man known to none of the others. The monks of St. Disibod sent him, he said. If so, it was to destroy the work of God. Embrich! Hold him, fellows! Don't let him run!"

"Get your hands off me!" Embrich protested as the men nearest dragged him forward. "I haven't done anything!"

"You are the worst mason I even saw in my life," Ludwig said. "An apprentice on his first day would make fewer mistakes."

There was a murmur of agreement from the men.

Hildegarde faced the man.

"Your brother workers condemn you," she said. "Have you nothing to say for yourself? You know that, if it is proven that you caused Albrecht's death, you will hang."

"I did nothing!" Embrich drew himself up. "It's true that I lied to be hired on here, but not to stop the building, at least, not like that."

"Yes, I know." The prioress sat on the folding chair one of the servants had brought. "You are here because of my daughter, Trauchte."

Embrich's jaw dropped. Hildegarde continued.

"You will not win her, no matter how unhappy she is here," she informed him. "She is a professed nun. Your soul would be forfeit if you stole her away. Does her father know about your disguise?"

"No, my lady." Embrich's shoulders drooped. "I overheard him telling a friend that Trauchte hated Rupertsberg and he was going to get her. I thought that might mean that she would consider me again."

"Foolish man!" Hildegarde shook her head. "She is pledged to a Heavenly Bridegroom who will care for her in this world and the next. What have you to offer her to compare with that?"

As Embrich was hunting for a response, Sister Richardis came from the guest house. She leaned over and said something softly to the prioress.

"Good," Hildegarde told her. "Bring him here."

A few moments later Peter and Margaret arrived, escorting a man who looked as if he would rather be anywhere else. Embrich took one look at him and blanched.

Hildegarde gave him a withering look. "Lord Gerlac," she said. "If you wished to visit Trauchte you could have applied at the gate."

"She feared that you wouldn't let me see her," Gerlac answered. "My lady." He fell to his knees before her. "I wish only the best for her. She is not meant for conditions such as these."

Hildgarde regarded him with loathing. "Good fruit comes only from good seed. Your seed is full of tares. By appealing to you, Trauchte has shown herself unfit to associate with my daughters here. Her soul, and yours, may be saved only by deep penitence."

"Take your daughter," she ordered. "Trauchte is mine no longer."

Lord Gerlac stood. "It is not God but Satan who speaks through you, woman! I'll make sure no girl is ever entrusted to you again."

He turned to go.

"Lord Gerlac!" Hildegarde called after him. "Take your servant, as well."

He turned around slowly.

"What are you talking about?" he asked.

"Ludwig." The prioress beckoned to him.

The master mason looked in terror from Gerlac to Hildegarde and back.

"What madness is this?" he asked. "My lady, I am a master mason!"

"That you are," she said. "And your last assignment was the chapel at Lord Gerlac's family monastery."

She turned back to Gerlac.

"You hired him to see to it that I abandoned God's plan to establish a house here," she accused him. "You are equally guilty of his crimes. I shall be writing the archbishop to inform him of your deeds. I've no doubt that he will feel obliged to report them to the emperor."

"This is nonsense," Gerlac sputtered. "I know nothing of this man or his crimes."

"I've done nothing!" Ludwig insisted. "It was Embrich; you know it was. He wanted the convent to fail so he could rescue his beloved."

Hildegarde shook her head. "As you have often said, Embrich doesn't have the skill to hammer a nail. He wouldn't know how to create such perfect ruin. Lord Edgar?"

"My lady," Edgar bowed. "As you bade me, I examined the materials that had been damaged. The work was skillfully done to cause the most disruption. The only exception was the board that broke under the worker, Albrecht. I think it was intended only to crack, but he must have landed on it harder than anticipated."

Ludwig started to protest once more. Edgar held up his hand.

"I couldn't be certain that you were doing it," he said. "But, when my wife fell, I watched you. Others came to help her. You ran to retrieve the hide she slipped on. You had greased it, hadn't you?"

"Of course not!" he shouted. "You can't lay this on me. My lord!" He appealed to Gerlac.

"I don't know this man" Gerlac put on his gloves. "Whatever he has done is of his own design."

"You bastard!" Ludwig screamed.

Lord Gerlac's eyes dared Hildegarde to try to detain him. She considered him a moment, then waved him away.

"Heaven will see to your punishment," she stated confidently. "Go."

When Lord Gerlac and his weeping daughter had left and a still sputtering Ludwig been locked in the gatehouse to await the judgment of the bishop, Hildegarde summoned Catherine, Edgar, Margaret and Peter to the gatehouse.

"I am grateful for your aid," she told them. "I had suspected Ludwig for some time, but needed someone from the outside to create a situation that would allow me to accuse him. Lord Gerlac may have hired him, but the abbot of Disibod recommended him as well. If I sent him packing, it would have been an insult, and relations between us are difficult already."

"It was little enough to do, *Magistra*," Edgar said. "A bit of playacting."

"I thought I fell quite realistically," Catherine added. "I've had practice."

Edgar took Margaret's hand. "I am ready to give you my treasured sister. I know she will blossom here."

Margaret was trembling, but nodded agreement.

Hildegarde shook her head.

"She is not meant for the convent," she said. "In my visions I have seen her standing in the breath of the north wind, struggling to overcome its force. I have seen the warm wind of the south wrap itself around her in protection. I have not seen her reciting the Divine Office."

"But, but . . ." Catherine was totally taken aback. "Do you think her unworthy?"

"No, my child," Hildegarde sighed and held out her hand to Margaret. "You are bright and pious and obedient, all I could wish. I fear that your life would be easier if I took you in, but the Living Light has another path for you. I am sorry."

Margaret couldn't believe it.

"But I must marry," she said. "If not Christ, then whom?"

Behind her, Peter's face shone with hope.

Hildegarde kissed Margaret's cheek.

"Have faith, my child," she said. "An answer will present itself. You have done me a great service. When the north wind beats against you, send word and I shall pray for the south wind to find you. This I promise."

And with that, Margaret had to be content.

The Deadly Bride

We now turn to two stories I wrote about Solomon, Edgar's business partner. Anne Perry asked me to write a story based on a book of the Bible for Thou Shalt Not Kill *published by Carroll & Graf in 2006. Being contrary, I chose the book of Tobit, which is part of the Apocrypha. It's a strange story and I have followed it to some extent. Solomon is the sort of person who doesn't accept a supernatural reason for something if he can find a human one. In this he is not that unusual for a medieval person.*

July 1140

The summer sun was setting on Paris. The air was full of the sound of mothers calling children home, of bells calling monks to prayer and of beer casks being tapped for workers thirsty from a day in the heat.

Solomon ben Jacob stretched his legs out into the narrow street and balanced his drinking bowl on the wooden bench next to him. A stray dog sniffed at the contents and Solomon growled at it, but without energy. The evening was too hot to begrudge a fellow creature a swallow of beer.

The benches were becoming crowded but no one took the seat next to him. Jews were tolerated in Paris, but few people wanted to associate with them. Solomon closed his eyes and leaned back against the tavern wall, grateful to be left alone.

A moment later he was alarmed to feel the shadow of someone standing above him. He sat up, alert at once. The slanting rays of the sun outlined a slightly-built man with a heavy beard. He exhaled in relief. It was his old friend, Tobias.

"Solomon! Rejoice with me!" Tobias sat down with a thump that rocked the bench. "I'm getting married!"

"*Mazel tov!*" Solomon lifted his bowl and drank. "Better you than me. Who is she? Did your mother find her for you?"

"No," Tobias said proudly. "I arranged the marriage myself."

Solomon blinked in surprise. "And your families don't mind? Amazing! Who is she? Do I know her?"

"Probably not," Tobias answered. "She lives in Rouen."

"I don't go there much," Solomon admitted. "You couldn't find a girl closer to home?"

Tobias' stricken look made Solomon wish he'd held his tongue. A poor man with a blind father and aging mother to care for had little chance for a suitable bride.

"Well, I wish you a long and happy life with her," he said quickly, signaling the pot boy for another bowl of beer. "Are you moving there or bringing her back here to Paris?"

Tobias wiggled uncomfortably on the bench.

Solomon put the bowl down. He turned to look at his friend.

"Tobias," he sighed. "I know what you're going to ask. I'm not going with you all the way to Rouen to pick up your bride."

"Why not?" Tobias bristled. "You're my best friend. Who else would I want to witness my wedding?"

"I have to be in Toulouse then." Solomon said the first thing he could think of.

"No you don't," Tobias countered. "I already asked your uncle. And I didn't tell you when it would be."

He put his arm around Solomon's shoulder. "Please come with me. Meet my Sarah. Dance at the wedding feast. Who knows, you may find a wife of your own among her friends."

Solomon gave a snort. "My aunt Johanna has already combed all of Normandy, France and Champagne searching for a bride for me."

He closed his eyes. Sarah of Rouen: the name stirred something in his memory. Suddenly, he remembered.

"*Adonai!* Tobias, you can't mean the daughter of Raguel the linen merchant?"

Tobias lifted his chin. "As a matter of fact, yes. She's beautiful, pious, intelligent and kind. I'm fortunate that her parents have allowed the match."

Solomon was aghast. "Beautiful, pious, intelligent and cursed, Tobias! Has no one told you about her? You'll not live out your wedding night."

Tobias pulled away from Solomon. "I thought you were more rational than that," he said. "How can you believe the slanders about her?"

"Slanders?" Solomon's voice rose. "Three times her father has married her off and three men have died before bedding her. That's not rumor; it's fact."

"Solomon, quiet!" Tobias looked nervously at the men drinking and talking around them.

He moved closer to Solomon and spoke in a tense whisper.

"I don't believe Sarah is cursed," he said. "And I don't believe she killed those men as some say."

"And what is your explanation?" Solomon asked with a cynical grimace. "Her husbands all expired from anticipation?"

"No," Tobias answered seriously. "I believe that the Lord, blessed be He, laid His hand upon them so that she might be saved for me."

Solomon's jaw dropped.

"You see yourself as a divinely appointed husband?" He snorted his opinion of that.

Tobias smiled. "How else could I have become betrothed to her? Since my father lost his sight, my mother and I have been hard pressed to survive and care for him. I am a man without money or prospects. Sarah's father is rich. She is his only child. If not for the belief in this curse, many men would be begging for her hand."

"You're mad," Solomon observed.

Tobias hung his head. "This is my only chance. I must care for my parents in their last years. Sarah's father will support them as well as us," he said. "I'm honored that he has even considered my request. Why aren't you willing to celebrate with me?"

The idea of being happy for Tobias' imminent death was so ridiculous that Solomon refused to continue the discussion. He finished his beer and left his friend to his dreams of matrimony.

But the young man wasn't so quickly discouraged. The next morning he appeared at the door of the house where Solomon lived with his aunt Johanna and uncle Eleazar.

"May the Lord bless all here," he greeted them.

"Thank you, Tobias," Eleazar smiled. "May He keep you and your parents in good health. Come, sit down."

Johanna made a place for him and handed him a bowl to wash his hands from before passing him the platter of soft cheese covered in fruit.

"Solomon told us your news," she said. "Your parents are happy with this match?"

Tobias nodded, his mouth full. "Sarah's mother is a cousin on my father's side. She has been unfortunate in her marriages, nothing more. Why should she be cursed?"

"Being good and pious can't protect one from the evil in the world," Johanna said. "Look at your poor father. He didn't deserve blindness. It is not our place to ask why the Holy One, blessed be He, allows such things to happen."

"Exactly," Tobias answered. "Why should we assume a curse? It is just as possible that the Lord was saving Sarah for me."

He turned to Solomon. "Whatever you think of the marriage, won't you come with me for the sake of friendship?"

Eleazar coughed. "I do have a small task that you might do for me in Rouen, if you wouldn't mind."

Solomon gave him a sour look. He sighed and threw up his hands.

"Very well," he said. "I suppose I should go to the shops and look for a bridal gift. I only hope you survive to enjoy it."

Tobias left to prepare. Solomon went down to sit at the riverbank, chewing on a blade of grass. His thoughts were sour. Everything he had heard seemed to support the belief that some otherworldly hand had struck down Sarah's first three husbands. If that were so then there was no way from keeping Tobias from death. Solomon knew that the scholars would say it was the height of pride to assume that man can understand divine judgments. But he had lived too long among the questioning students of Paris, both Jewish and Christian. They accepted a supernatural reason only when all the natural ones had been eliminated.

Had anyone bothered to seek a human hand in all this?

Solomon gave a deep sigh. It appeared that he had been divinely appointed to find out.

In the study hall of the synagogue in the town of Rouen, there was equal consternation.

"Raguel has betrothed Sarah yet again?" Peretz nearly blotted the scroll he was copying. "What man would be so rash?"

"I don't know," his fellow student Shemariah answered. "Don't tip over the inkpot. Master Samuel is unhappy enough with your work as it is."

Peretz set the pot to one side and carefully covered the scroll to dry.

"Now, tell me," he demanded. "Who would marry Sarah after she was thrice widowed? More importantly, will there be another wedding feast?"

Shemariah laughed. "Always ready to fill your belly!"

"Raguel has good wine and sets a fine table," Peretz answered, laughing too. "Why shouldn't I enjoy it, as long as I'm not the groom?"

"Shh!" Shemariah cautioned.

Another man had just entered the house of study. He was in his late thirties and his dark hair was deciding whether to turn gray or just finish falling out. The beard was decidedly gray, and these things together made him seem a generation older than his years.

"Samuel!" Peretz greeted him. "Is it true that your cousin Sarah will again be a bride?"

"So my uncle tells me." Samuel shook his head. "How he can keep doing this to the poor girl, I don't know. It's clear that the Holy One, blessed be He, does not intend for Sarah to marry."

"I've heard it said that a demon comes into the chamber and strangles her husbands as soon as they approach the bed," Peretz commented.

"That's nonsense!" Samuel rounded on him. "My family has does not harbor demons."

"Of course not," Peretz apologized quickly, seeing his chance for an invitation slipping away. "It was only idle gossip, I'm sure. She must have been cursed by someone with a grudge against her father. When will the wedding be?"

"As soon as the groom arrives from Paris," Samuel told them. "If reason doesn't prevail. When I've finished here, I'm going to go see if I can convince Uncle Raguel not to put Sarah through this again."

"What does she think about it?" Shemariah asked quietly.

Peretz glanced at him. He had forgotten that Shemariah had been one of Sarah's earliest suitors. Raguel had rejected him as not being of good enough family. Did he still have hopes for her?

Samuel shrugged. "I haven't seen her. But she doesn't have much choice, after all. It's not as if she could be sent off to a convent like the Christians do with their unwanted women."

Shemariah tensed at this depiction of Sarah, but said nothing. Soon after, both he and Samuel left. Peretz rolled up the now dry scroll. His face was unusually serious. Even after the mysterious deaths of Sarah's husbands, Shemariah had renewed his offer for her. Peretz was wondering just what lengths a man would go to have the woman he loved.

Tobias and Solomon had taken the river Seine all the way to Rouen. Despite his worry over the fate of his friend, Solomon had enjoyed the voyage, doing nothing but lie out of the way on the barge as it took wine casks down to the coast to be put on a ship for England. They reached the town late on a Friday afternoon. Tobias had fretted the last few bends of the river, fearing that they wouldn't arrive before the start of Shabbat. But there had been time to unload their baggage and take it to the home of Bonnevie, the wealthiest Jew in town, who had agreed to put them up until the wedding.

Solomon was happy to have the Sabbath meal with them but not so enthusiastic about accompanying Tobias and Bonnevie to the synagogue for prayers first. Fortunately, there were enough men in the community that he had only to try to stay awake and keep his stomach from rumbling until the end.

He took the time to observe the other men of the minyan. The two students, Peretz and Shemariah, prayed with closed eyes, apparently interested in nothing but their devotions. The cousin of Raguel, Samuel, seemed distracted. Well, Solomon thought, not everyone could shed his worries upon entering the house of prayer. The bride's father, Raguel, also had difficulty concentrating. Bonnevie read the portion in tones as rich as his purse. He seemed to have no thoughts other than impressing the Lord with his piety. The other men were much like those of Paris. Solomon had a hard time imagining that any of them was concealing murder in his heart.

That evening, Bonnevie took Solomon aside.

"Tobias is a good man," he stated.

"Yes," Solomon said. "Devoted to his parents."

"An only son," Bonnevie said sadly. "How can they send him to this?"

"I don't know," Solomon answered. "Perhaps they don't believe he is in danger. This curse seems to be assumed by everyone, but why? How exactly did the other men die?"

Bonnevie's usually genial expression changed. "They simply stopped breathing," he said. "At least, that's all we can tell. The first time the man was a great deal older than Sarah." He gave an embarrassed grin. "We all assumed that the prospect of a young bride was too much for him. The second man was about your age. A scholar from a good family. He collapsed on the way to the bridal chamber. His limbs seemed to freeze. He died before morning."

"After that, I'm surprised there was a third," Solomon commented.

Bonnevie shrugged. "Raguel is very rich and his daughter very beautiful. More than that. Sarah is kind and pious. She doesn't deserve to be cursed in this way."

He shook his head and sighed, then continued. "The third marriage was about three years ago. A man from London. I don't know much about him. He seemed fine, although he drank more at the wedding supper than a bridegroom should. That was the worst. He and Sarah were alone. She says that he started to reach for her, then stopped as if struck. She screamed. He was dead before she could bring help. His expression was of a man in a nightmare, twisted in horror. That was when the rumors began. "

"Well, if she isn't murdering them herself, I don't see how anyone else could be," Solomon concluded. "Curse or human hands, Tobias shouldn't be allowed to marry her until we know for certain."

Bonnevie agreed. "Excellent!" he smiled. "And how do you propose we do that?"

Solomon had no idea. "I'll sleep on the matter," he told his host. "Perhaps the Holy One will send me the answer in a dream."

The object of all this concern was the one most upset about the prospect of marriage. Sarah, daughter of Raguel and Edna, still a virgin and likely to remain one, was trying to think of a way out.

"Mother," she said. "I am not going to be a widow again. How can you continue to try to marry me off? It's clear that the Lord doesn't wish me to be any man's wife."

The two women were sitting in the enclosed garden behind their home. Sarah's mother took great pride in the arrangement of the flower beds and the fact that she had managed to get a pomegranate to survive in Normandy. But neither Sarah nor Edna was taking any joy in the fragrant roses or the struggling little tree.

Edna leaned over and cupped Sarah's face in her hands.

"My exquisite child," she smiled sadly. "We cannot know the desires of the Holy One. It may be, as Tobias believes, that He was guarding you for him alone. In that case, everything will be fine."

Sarah pulled away. "And I am simply to have faith that I won't have to watch Tobias die, too? Mother, listen to your words! If Father weren't so respected in the community, we'd have been driven out by now. I am Sarah the thrice-cursed and that's only what they say when I'm there to overhear. I'm not going to risk Tobias' life on a foolish hope."

She stood and turned her back to her mother. Edna sighed. Everything Sarah said was true. Perhaps in her eagerness to see her daughter married she was going against the Divine plan. How was one to know?

Sarah turned around.

"Mother, have you ever asked yourself why this is happening?" she demanded. "Who could hate me this much? Who could care so little about the lives of three men?"

"I'm not a fool, daughter!" Edna snapped back. "Your father and I have searched our lives for anyone we might have wronged. We would gladly make amends if this evil could be removed from you. But we can think of nothing. It's as if a demon has been loosed upon us."

Sarah knelt next to Edna and wrapped her arms about her.

"Mother, we must not put Tobias in the way of this demon." Her voice shook.

Edna tilted Sarah's face up. What she saw made her heart shudder.

"Oh, my dearest!" she cried. "Don't tell me that you have fallen in love with this man? You mustn't let any one know. If someone has laid a curse upon you, this will only make them more determined to destroy us."

Sarah burst into sobs. "I know. I know! Mother, please, you must stop my wedding!"

Edna stroked her hair. "It's too late, my darling. The *ketuba* has been signed. We can't cancel it now."

Three days in Rouen had convinced Solomon that Raguel was widely envied for his wealth and despised for his flaunting of it. More than one person had confided that Sarah was too much prized by her parents.

"She's their idol," one woman sneered. "The way they bedeck her, you'd think she was Queen Esther herself."

Only Bonnevie had nothing bad to say of him. "Raguel is an honest man, for all he drives a hard bargain."

"Is there anyone who may have been ruined by one of these bargains?" Solomon persisted.

"No one I know of," Bonnevie answered. "'Even so, what point would there be in killing three men? Why not just kill Raguel, if you have a grudge against him? And there's still the problem of how it was done. Until you can explain that, people will prefer to believe in a curse."

Solomon had no answer. He decided to take his concerns directly to Tobias' prospective in-laws.

Raguel greeted him with quiet cheer.

"You are Tobias' friend," he said. "We are delighted that you could come. I only wish his parents had been well enough to make the journey.

"Yes, so do I," Solomon answered. He tried to think of a way to introduce the subject of murder without committing a social blunder. "They are happy to welcome Sarah into their family and hope she and Tobias will soon return to Paris."

"Papa, who is our guest?"

Solomon turned to look. Sarah stood in the doorway to the garden. Her arms were full of flowers. She smiled.

"Ah," Solomon inhaled sharply. Now he understood. Sarah was more than beautiful. She was radiant. Even without a dowry, she would be a prize for any man. It was also clear why people preferred to blame the deaths on a curse. No one could see her gentle, sad face and believe her a murderer.

Raguel introduced Solomon.

"Have you come to tell us that Tobias wishes to be released?" she asked. "If so, I shall gladly agree, for his sake."

This took Solomon aback.

"He doesn't know I'm here," he explained. "I only came to . . . to . . . I'm sorry."

He bowed to take his leave. Sarah held up a hand to stop him.

"I understand," she said. "You're his friend. It's your duty to try to save him from this fate."

"I see now why he rushes to embrace it," Solomon took her out-stretched hand. "Do you think you are cursed?"

"Oh, yes," Sarah answered. "What other answer is there?"

She looked up at him. He had never seen such an expression of despair. His heart sank. If Sarah and her family had no idea what was happening, there seemed to be no way to find out. Now he had to face Tobias and admit he had failed.

Tobias was stubborn in his refusal to break his betrothal.

"Tobias, they are offering to release you from the marriage contract," Solomon told his friend. "You will lose no honor. Do it. Tear up the *ketuba* and let's go home."

Tobias drew himself up proudly. "I would never do that!" he stated. "What kind of a man would I be if I abandoned Sarah?"

"A live one?" Solomon was losing patience. "I'll grant you she's a great marriage prize. After Bonnevie, Raguel is the richest man in town. But how many times must I remind you that you won't enjoy it if you're dead?"

They were standing near the wharf, watching people and goods being unloaded. There was a cool breeze blowing from the water. It brought a smell of fish and rotting plants. It reminded Solomon that he could be sitting on a log next to the Seine in Paris swilling wine with his friends, instead of in Rouen trying to knock sense into Tobias.

Tobias had answered him, but Solomon's mind was far up river.

"What?" he asked.

"I said that the men from the Yeshiva, Peretz and Shemariah, are giving a dinner for me tonight, since I have no family here," Tobias repeated. "Will you come with me?"

"If I must," Solomon replied, still staring at the river. Suddenly, he had a thought.

"Tobias," he asked, "did all the other bridegrooms have a dinner the night before the wedding?"

Tobias lifted his shoulders. "I don't know. It's traditional. Why?"

"Nothing," Solomon answered. "Just promise that you won't start without me."

"That's better!" Tobias grinned. "Just don't make me wait."

Solomon walked back to the home of Raguel and Edna. He needed to get more information.

Raguel was annoyed by Solomon's question.

"Of course we considered poison," he said. "We're not credulous peasants. But the men didn't become ill. They didn't vomit or clutch their stomachs. They simply stopped breathing as if frozen. And, even if it were poison, who could have given it to all those men?" Raguel continued. "And how could it have been done?"

"At the dinner the night before the wedding or at the wedding supper," Solomon explained.

Edna disagreed. "That would be impossible. The food at the dinner is served from common platters and shared. On the wedding night, the bride and groom sip from the same wine cup and share a trencher. You aren't suggesting anything that hasn't been considered."

"Oh." Solomon shook his head. He should have known it wasn't that simple. "Very well. I know you say you have wronged no one intentionally. But there is no one without enemies."

Raguel admitted this. "Of course there are those who say I took trade from them, but they were not asked to Sarah's weddings. Without sorcery, they could not have harmed anyone there. And how can we prove such a thing?"

Once again defeated, Solomon went back to Bonnevie's home to prepare for the dinner. He wondered how soon he'd be preparing for a funeral.

Under the circumstances, the feast for the bridegroom didn't have the ribald tone of others that Solomon had attended. But the wine pitcher went around with great frequency and the water pitcher rarely followed it. As the evening progressed, the tension began to release itself in bursts of maudlin poetry and song. Solomon realized that the men, unable to celebrate the impending tragedy of the wedding, had switched to Spanish songs of love lost, of Israel lost. Tobias was singing and weeping along with them. A cheerful gathering, indeed.

Solomon had let the pitcher pass him by, a sacrifice that he hoped Tobias would appreciate. He watched the others with the clarity and repugnance of the sober. The students, Peretz and Shamariah, were gulping down tears. Bonnevie had fallen asleep, his head on his arms like a child at a Seder. Raguel and his nephew, Samuel, were sitting on either side of Tobias, all three staring into a wine cup as if at an oracle.

Shamariah pushed himself off his stool and staggered over to Tobias.

"Yrrr a good man," he said with a hiccough. "Go home and frrrget Sarrrah. The Holy One . . ."

"Blessed be He," Bonnevie murmured from the table top.

"Blessssssed be He," Shamariah agreed. "He doesn't want our Sarrrah to wed. It's cleearrrr. Go home, Tobias."

He slowly folded to the ground at Tobias' feet.

Samuel stared at the crumpled form, shaking his head.

"Never mind him, Tobias," he said. "Shamariah just wants her for himself. It would never happen."

Raguel was now weeping on Samuel's shoulder.

"My sweet Sarah," he burbled. "My only child. The light of my house. And Tobias, the only son of his good parents. What a joy it would be to share a grandson with Tobit! How can we keep tragedy from them?"

"There, there, Uncle," Samuel patted him. "Whatever comes, I shall see that Sarah is taken care of."

"And I," came Shamariah's voice from the floor.

Raguel sniffed back tears. "Thank you, my friends."

Solomon stared at them. Ordinarily, he would have been just as drunk, seeing the world through a soft haze. Now suddenly, everything came into focus. They had been asking the wrong questions all along. There was really only one reason for each one of Sarah's husbands to die before the marriage could be consummated. And, when he knew why, he knew who. It was the how that still eluded him.

One thing he was certain of: Tobias was still in great danger.

The wedding day was cloudy with a cool breeze. In the house of Bonnevie, only Solomon was awake to eat the bread and fruit the servants had left for them. He paced the hall until his host finally appeared, bleary-eyed and disheveled.

"Bonnevie!" Solomon greeted him. "I need to ask you something at once."

Bonnevie gave him a poisonous glance. "Only if you lower your voice," he said.

Solomon apologized. "I only need to know something about Raguel's finances. What happens to his money if Sarah dies childless?"

"It would go to his wife, Edna, and then to the children of his brothers." Bonnevie winced. "You could have figured that out for yourself."

"Yes," Solomon said. "I just wanted to be sure. I need to go out for a while. Don't let anyone near Tobias until I return, please."

"Anything." Bonnevie waved him away. "Just remove your all-too-energetic self from my sight."

He sat down and rested his head in his hands as Solomon tiptoed out.

Solomon spent the day asking more questions as delicately as he could. It was one thing to think a man a murderer, another to prove it. His inquiries led him finally to a Christian apothecary, who remembered both the man and the remedy he had purchased.

"I warned him that only a small pinch is necessary," the apothecary explained. "In wine is best; it kills the flavor. The whole packet could kill, but I'm sure the buyer was very careful. He's been back four times in the past six years or so. So the concoction must have given satisfaction."

"What is the herb that can harm?" Solomon asked.

"Ah, good old hemlock," the man smiled. "The plant grows everywhere. Sometimes people mistake it for parsley, but a bite or two and they know their mistake. A small dose makes one ill but no more. But it's only in combination with my secret ingredient that the desired effect occurs."

Solomon thanked him and hurried back to find Tobias. He wondered why the murderer hadn't made the poisonous compound himself. Then it occurred to him that if he had been discovered he could blame the Christian. Although going back four times would be harder to explain.

Tobias was relieved to see him.

"It's almost time for the wedding," he exclaimed. "Hurry and change. I can't let Sarah think I'm reluctant."

"Yes, in a minute," Solomon answered. "Tobias, has anyone given you something to take, just in case you have trouble, um, with the consummation?"

"How did you guess?" Tobias laughed, holding up a small bag. "Can you imagine? I've done nothing but dream of this night for months. I'll need no help from anyone but Sarah. Don't say anything, though. I don't want to hurt his feelings. It was a generous thought."

Solomon promised.

The wedding, though subdued, went smoothly. Sarah and Tobias sat together at the dinner afterward looking at each other in a way that gave Solomon a pang of jealousy. He prayed that he was right and that no harm would come to Tobias in the night.

The new couple were led to their chamber and told to bolt the door on the inside. The windows were small and high in the wall. At least Solomon felt certain no one could enter.

The next morning, half the community was outside Raguel's house.

"Are they awake yet?" Shemariah asked when Edna came to the door. "Is Sarah all right?"

"Has the curse been broken?" Samuel was next to him.

Solomon worked his way through to stand just behind the two men.

"Shame on you all for wanting to awaken a newly married couple at dawn," Edna said. "The door is still shut and I've heard no sound this morning. But in this case, perhaps we should check. If we knock and hear Tobias' voice, will you all go home?"

Solomon grabbed Shemariah and Samuel and volunteered to go with her.

The three men approached the door.

"I feel very awkward doing this," Shemariah said.

"Sarah may need your support if the curse has struck again," Samuel reminded him.

Solomon raised his hand to knock. The door flew open. In the threshold stood Tobias and Sarah both radiantly alive.

Samuel stepped back. "That can't be!" He pointed at Tobias. "So it was you who killed the others! This proves it!"

Solomon caught Samuel's outstretched hand and twisted his behind his back.

"It proves nothing except that Tobias didn't feel the need of your potion to enjoy his wedding night," he announced to the people who were now crowding into the hall.

"What are you talking about?" Raguel demanded. "Samuel is Sarah's cousin."

"Exactly," Solomon answered. "And he has a wife and children, but not much money. It was only when I stopped seeing this as a crime of revenge or passion that I saw the obvious. Sarah is the only child. If she dies too soon, then Raguel might do anything with his wealth. But if she were convinced never to marry, then her inheritance would go to Samuel's family."

"That's ridiculous!" Samuel cried. "I would never have anything to do with demons. I didn't curse her."

"Demons, no," Solomon said. "There was never a curse. Just a nice aphrodisiac for a nervous groom."

He produced the packet.

"Only I wasn't nervous," Tobias grinned. "Was I, Sarah? Samuel gave me the herbs. He told me to pour wine over them and drink the whole mess down. It was really clever. I wouldn't have guessed if Solomon hadn't explained it to me. If you can't put poison into a man's cup, get him to put it there himself."

"Lies! All of it!" Samuel screamed. "I only wanted to help. That Christian must have tainted it. They don't care if we die."

"What Christian?" Raguel asked. "You don't mean Silas down by the bridge? I think we should have a word with him. Solomon, you can release my nephew now. The community will decide if he is guilty."

"Gladly." Solomon pushed Samuel into the arms of the crowd. "My only care was to see that Tobias didn't meet the same fate as the other bridegrooms."

Sarah stepped forward. "I don't know how to thank you," she said. "I only wish you could be as happy as we are. I have a friend..."

Solomon didn't hear the end of the sentence. He made his escape and was soon on his way home, far from marriage arrangements and deadly brides.

Solomon's Decision

I wrote this story in 1997 for the anthology Crime Through Time, *which I edited with Miriam Grace Monfredo. It's not set in any particular year: 1143 will do, if you need to fix it. The idea for it came from an interest in the mystic side of Jewish philosophy. The Kabbala had not been composed at this time, but the seeds were there. I had also been reading about the reality of life for Jews under Muslim rule. As with most myths, that of one big happy family of monotheists living in Spain and producing great strides in science is only partly true. For one thing, the more secular the society, the more religious toleration there was. At the time of this story, the Almoravids ruled Andalusia. They had become somewhat easy-going since they had conquered the Arabs there before them. In 1146 the "corrupt" Islamic rulers were conquered by fundamentalist Almohads from North Africa. They were much harder on those not Muslim. Many Spanish Jews fled, some to France, others, like the family of Maimonides, went to Egypt. This story takes place in the last years of the Almoravids, when relations were still good among the practitioners of the three religions.*

———

Yishmael ibn Samuel leaned back onto the pillows covering the steps down to his walled garden, gave a deep sigh and reached for his wine cup.

"I am in constant torment," he said as he emptied the cup and held it out for a slave to refill. "My soul is devoured by longing, my heart is pierced by a thousand arrows, my eyes are blinded by bitter tears . . ."

"And your bowels are rumbling from the dinner you just inhaled," his friend finished for him.

Yishmael looked at him reproachfully.

"Solomon ben Jacob, you men of Ashkenaz have no poetry," he said. "Have you never been in love?"

"Often," Solomon replied. "But my Aunt Johanna has a tonic she gives me for it. Shall I have her send you a flask?"

Yishmael laughed shortly and shook his head. "No tonic can cool the fire in my body. In Paris, perhaps, you are all so numbed by the cold that your passion is easily quenched. But here in Córdoba we know what it is to suffer the pain of desire."

He stretched out his hand and plunged it into a bowl of chopped fruit mixed with honey and almonds. He ate messily, licked the mixture from his palm and then waved his sticky hand above his head until another slave appeared with a bowl of scented water and a drying cloth.

Solomon yawned. The winter night came later in Córdoba than at home and the wind was gentler. It was pleasant to sit in the garden drinking wine, knowing that a soft bed awaited. He supposed the comfort was worth the tedium of listening to Yishmael go on about his latest obsession. All the same, he was relieved when a voice called from the doorway.

"*Abba,* are you going to keep poor Solomon up all night? He's only just arrived and must be exhausted from his journey."

Both men looked up at the shape silhouetted in the light from the dining hall. Only Mayah dared chastise her father publicly. Solomon smiled at her, both in gratitude at the interruption and in appreciation of Mayah herself, standing with her back to the lamplight, her body outlined underneath her white cotton robe. Mayah noticed the leer beneath the smile and moved quickly down the steps into the shadows.

"Solomon, have you nothing better to do than encourage my father to eat and drink too much? Doesn't your uncle expect you to work while you're here? And what about that abbot who hired you? I hear he's eternally impatient to acquire more jewels to ornament the idols in his church."

"I see why your father can't find you a husband," Solomon grumped. "You nag like an old woman. Not that it's any of your affair, Mayah, but I've been working since I arrived in Spain last week, searching out perfectly matched rubies for that blasted abbot's altarpiece and trying to convince a goldsmith to return to Paris with me in the nastiest, coldest part of the year so that the church of St. Denis will have a gold statue of one of their *desfaé* saints with real rubies in the wounds in time for the feast of whatever saint it is."

Solomon upended his wine cup unto his mouth but the slave had refilled it when he wasn't looking and the wine spilled out, into his nose and down his clean tunic.

Mayah gave a snort and a sharp nod.

"Serves you right for doing business with idolaters," she said.

Yishmael intervened. "Now, now, Mayah. You forget that my trading with Solomon and those idolaters paid for your new necklace and that book of philosophy you wanted so much."

His daughter bowed her head, not in submission, but contemplation. After a moment she spoke again, more gently.

"My father is correct," she admitted. "I have no right to berate you for doing what is necessary to survive as a Jew in Edom."

Solomon had been occupied with blowing his nose and wiping his face and so missed her words, but he caught the apology in her tone.

"It's nothing," he mumbled. "You were right; it's been a long journey. I'm extremely tired. Could you show me to my bed?"

Mayah led him to an alcove where a bed had been made up behind silk curtains that shimmered in the light of the oil lamp she held.

Solomon put a hand on her arm. "Before you go, Mayah . . ."

She stiffened and her mouth opened as if to scream. Solomon moved away, startled.

"I'm sorry," he told her. "I meant you no harm. I only wanted to ask about this person your father is so taken with. Is it someone I know?"

"I'm sorry." She relaxed. "Some of my father's guests . . ." She collected herself. "Oh, yes, Father's new object of adoration. You may have met him, Moshe ibn Daud. He lives with his teacher, Gabriol ibn Yosef."

"Moshe," Solomon thought. "No, I don't remember him. What's he like? Does he know of your father's feelings?"

"That one?" Mayah laughed. "Half the men of Córdoba write love poems to him, even the Christians. And a good number of the women, as well. Father is simply one of his many admirers. I doubt Moshe cares. He's a serious scholar."

"I'm normally immune to the charms of young men," he commented. "But I'd like to meet this Moshe, if possible, just to see what the attraction is."

Mayah sighed. "He'll be here tomorrow for dinner, with his teacher. You can see him then."

Solomon settled into the soft mattress but, despite his exhaustion, he couldn't sleep. Mayah's reaction to his touch worried him. Her mother was dead and the responsibility of the house had fallen to her. Had Yishmael neglected to see that she was unprotected from the attentions of the men coming to his home? Yishmael entertained visitors from as far away as Alexandria and England. He delighted in the company of travelers and learned men. Solomon wondered if his host were careful to inquire into the character of those who appeared at his door.

Perhaps he should say something to his friend about it. The old man was blind where his daughter was concerned. He hadn't found her a husband yet, not because of her sharp tongue, but because he refused to part with her. In Yishmael's opinion, no man was worthy.

Solomon punched the cushions into a better shape. "I'd wager that if Elijah descended from heaven on a burning cloud and asked for her hand, Yishmael would find a reason to refuse him," he thought as he finally drifted into sleep.

The Arab city of Córdoba was cosmopolitan, sophisticated and wealthy. The Caliphs were a reflection of the city, comfortable enough to be tolerant of the Jewish and Christian minorities. As long as the *dhimmi* remembered that they were subject to the laws of Islam, they were allowed to move freely in society. And, over the fifty years of Almoravid rule, the laws of Islam were relaxed to the point where wine was common at any table and dining among men of all faiths was normal.

So the next evening Solomon wasn't surprised to see the Arab silk merchant Ali ibn Tibbon among the guests, as well as a Norman spice trader from Sicily, who immediately backed Solomon into a corner and proceeded to tell him about the reliability of delivery and the quality of goods he could provide.

"Cumin, cloves, cinnamon," he ticked them off on his fingers. "From India and beyond. Nard, rare incense. Your abbot would do well to trade with me. I not only give the best service but a tenth of my profit goes to the monks of St. Jean l'Eremite in Palermo. So part of his payment is returned to the church."

Solomon thought privately that Abbot Suger would rather all the profits went to his own church. He smiled politely and tried to edge away.

"Solomon, old friend!" Ali ibn Tibbon moved the Norman aside and gave Solomon a bear hug. "I haven't seen you in years. When did you become a dignified man with a beard? I must be getting old."

He drew Solomon away to the table.

"Thank you for rescuing me," Solomon whispered. "Who is that man? Why did Yishmael invite him?"

"His name is Roger, Ranulf, something like that." Ali dismissed him with a shrug. "He's like all the *Farangi*, no manners, no poetry in him. Only greed. I don't know how you can live among them."

"Not all the French are like him," Solomon answered. "Some of them . . ." he stopped, staring at the men who had just entered. "Who . . . is *that* Moshe?"

"Ah, yes," Ali went toward the new arrival with open arms. "Dear Moshe! I'm so glad to see you again. My sweet boy. Tell me you will sing for us tonight. I shall die of grief if you don't."

Moshe smiled shyly. "Of course," he said. "I'm honored that you wish to hear my simple music."

As he was engulfed by Ali, Moshe looked over his shoulder at Solomon. He winked. Solomon's jaw dropped.

Moshe was a striking young man of about eighteen, tall, with long limbs and graceful hands. He had great dark eyes with luxuriant lashes many women would have bartered their virtue for. Solomon could understand how he could enchant Córdoba, where beauty was adored and sought after in all things. But he wasn't what Solomon expected.

There was more in his face than charm. There was intelligence and humor and something else. It took Solomon a moment to recognize what was also in Moshe's expression, it was so out of place. Behind the shy smile lay fear. In the midst of all this adulation, the boy was terrified. It gave him a vulnerability that only increased his appeal.

A gong sounded, summoning them all to the table. Solomon followed the others slowly, confused and intrigued by what he had seen in Moshe's face.

Moshe was placed between Yishmael and his teacher, Gabriol. The others sat on large pillows at low tables placed in a circle. The food was brought in and conversation dwelt on the weather and the best time to prune roses, light topics conducive to good digestion.

It was only when the bowls of fruit and almonds and pitchers of sweet date wine were brought in that the voices were raised in serious discussion.

"Have you finished translating that manuscript of Pythagoras yet?" Ali asked Gabriol.

"Moshe and I have almost deciphered it," the scholar replied. "Moshe is very excited about some marginal notes he found."

He nodded to his student, who explained.

"One of the previous owners of the manuscript was apparently interested in using the theories of Pythagoras to chart the relation between the stars and the earth."

"Geomancy?" Roger (or Ranulf) had been listening. "That's dangerous. One degree off and you can destroy the entire design. I knew a monk once who dabbled in that. He was killed by a lightning bolt."

The others all stopped and looked at him.

"He was!" the Norman insisted. "The tree he was standing under is still there, all twisted and black."

Gabriol nodded sagely. "A point to remember, Moshe. No geomancy during thunderstorms."

"Yes, Master," Moshe said. He bent his head respectfully. Solomon guessed at the grin he was hiding.

Ranulf (or Roger) sensed that he was being mocked. His jaw tightened. Yishmael quickly signaled for more wine.

"You must return tomorrow afternoon and tell me more about what you've learned," he told Moshe. "The evening is too far gone for me to concentrate on natural philosophy. Perhaps you would care to sing for us instead?"

"Of course" Moshe rose and went to the entry, where he had left his harp. When he returned, he hesitated at the doorway.

"Rev Yishmael," he said. "Perhaps your guests would like to hear Mayah, as well. She and I have been practicing a poem by Bahya. I've put music to it."

"My daughter is not a dancing girl to entertain the public." Yishmael frowned.

"Neither is Moshe," Ali reminded him. "Come, we are all friends. I have heard that Mayah has a beautiful voice. It would be an honor to listen to her."

The other guests all murmured agreement. Grudgingly, Yismael agreed. He sent a servant for Mayah.

"She might not come," he warned them. "Sometimes that girl is as proud as Vashti."

But Mayah appeared almost at once, modestly dressed, her head covered. She bowed to the men and took her place next to Moshe, who plucked a note on the harp.

They sang together.

Solomon didn't understand the words. They were singing in Arabic and he knew only enough to transact business. It didn't matter. It must be a love song. Anything Mayah and Moshe sang would have to become one. Now Solomon understood why Mayah wasn't concerned by her father's infatuation. He looked around the room. Wasn't it obvious to all of them?

The two singers never looked at each other. Mayah kept her eyes downcast. But even their avoidance was a declaration. Yishmael was smiling proudly at his daughter and tapping his finger on the edge of his cup in time to the music. The others only showed pleasure at the entertainment.

When they finished, Mayah bowed to the guests and bade them good night. Moshe followed her to the hallway to replace his harp in its case. He was only gone a moment. Only Solomon noticed the quick tug he gave to adjust his tunic as he re-entered the room.

Moshe resumed his place amidst the praise of the men. He spent the rest of the evening sitting quietly, apparently intent upon absorbing the knowledge of his elders. Solomon, not that much older than Moshe, imitated his silence. But he heard little of what was said, occupied with worry for Mayah and Moshe. Was their attachment the source of his fear?

The next afternoon Solomon made a point of returning early. Moshe was there with Gabriol and the two men were deep in discussion with Yishmael. A scroll was unrolled on the table before them.

"You see?" Moshe ran his finger along a line. "This parallels the thought of Saadia Gaon and the Arab Brethren of Purity. And yet, the notes made here on Pythgoras give their teachings another dimension."

Yishmael squinted at the scroll. "I have no idea, Moshe, my *'ofer.*" He said gently. "I can make out the Hebrew here but I don't read Greek."

Master Gabriol shook his head. "Moshe, it's well known that Saadia and the Brethren knew of the philosophy of Pythagoras. But they were wise men, able to pick the truth from his gentile misunderstanding. You go too far, my son. You are trying to study beyond your years. Your beard should be gray before you even attempt to delve into the secrets of the *Shekinah.*"

"Yes, Master." Moshe took the rebuke mildly.

Gabriol gave him a reassuring pat on the shoulder. "Someday your wisdom will match your enthusiasm and you shall be a great scholar. But all things have their proper time. Now that we know what is in it, you must promise not to look at this work again until I say you're ready. This is dangerous philosophy. Even those who think themselves wise have lost their way and their souls in this mysticism."

They finally became aware of Solomon standing in the doorway. Yishmael greeted him warmly.

"I'm sure that's enough for today, Moshe, *zaby,*" he said. "Solomon has no interest in philosophy. Would you entertain him for a few moments while I discuss a business matter with your master?"

The two older men left and Solomon sat next to Moshe, who was studying the scroll feverishly before it was taken from him.

"I don't read Greek any more than I do Arabic," he told the boy. "But I have heard of geomancy. One marks random points on the earth and connects them according to some formula. The resulting number is supposed to be used to read the secrets of the stars and foretell the future. There are many in France who practice it." He paused. "I have found nothing to make me believe such nonsense."

Moshe wasn't offended. He grinned at Solomon. "It's not necessary to scratch points in the dirt, but it helps. Any surface will do," he said. "But this philosophy is more than simple divination, as I've tried to explain to my teacher. The Holy One, blessed be He, has sent the *Shekinah* to touch the minds of many, even the gentiles. While we of course are the chosen people, the others have received knowledge, too, only hidden and unclear. I believe it is our responsibility to find all the pieces of wisdom that have been scattered among the peoples of the earth. When we put them together, we will know the plan of the Almighty for man. Perhaps then it will be the time for the Messiah to come."

His eyes glowed much as they had the night before, when he allowed himself to look on Mayah. Solomon was impressed, but also nervous.

"There is a teacher in France who has ideas like yours," he warned Moshe. "He says that Plato had been granted a glimmer of the eternal truth by one of the Christian gods, the Holy Spirit, they call it. The man's writings were condemned last year at a council."

Moshe shrugged. "The *Farangi* are frightened of Truth. Look at how they treat you and the other Jews who live among them. We are civilized in Córdoba." He smiled at Solomon. "But I have been behaving as boorishly as they, lecturing you like this. I'm sorry. Would you care for some wine?"

Solomon was about to accept when Yishmael and Gabriol returned. The scholar and the student left soon after.

The door had barely closed when Yishmael turned to Solomon. "Didn't I tell you he was magnificent?" he said. "So beautiful and yet so modest. How I would like to have him near me always!"

"Why don't you marry him to Mayah?" Solomon suggested. "Then he could live in your home."

"Mayah! Are you mad?" Yishmael's eyes were wide with horror. "Moshe is beloved of half the men of Córdoba. Even that disgusting Norman asked Ali ibn Tibbon about kidnapping Moshe to sell to some caliph in the east. Do you think I would give my daughter to such a man?"

The twistings of southern minds were a puzzle to Solomon.

"Yishmael," he said. "I've heard all about the love poems composed for Moshe. But no one has told me whom he writes his poems to."

"What do you mean?" Yishmael answered sharply.

"Nothing," Solomon answered quickly. "I just wondered where Moshe's affections lie. Has he shown any interest in those who proposition him? Has there ever been any rumor of him being seen with another man, or woman for that matter?"

He left it there, but he could tell that he had set the older man's mind on a new path. He hoped it would lead to a betrothal for Mayah and Moshe.

"It must be the soft living here," Solomon thought as he went to bed that night. "I can't believe I'm indulging in matchmaking. What would Aunt Johanna say?"

Solomon was awakened deep into the night by shouts from the courtyard below. Throwing on a long robe, he grabbed the little oil lamp by the door and hurried down to see what was happening.

There was no moon and the flicker from his small lamp did not reach far. In his rush to get to the source of the commotion, Solomon stepped on something left in the grass. He cried out in pain and bent to see what it was.

"Who put that there?"

Someone had left a thin stick poking only a few inches out of the ground, like a newly planted rose bush. But this was dead wood, pointed where it had entered the earth and notched near the top. Solomon yanked it up in annoyance and went on.

As he came around the corner, his eyes were dazzled by the light of a dozen torches. As his vision adjusted, he saw Yishmael kneeling in the middle of a group of men. He was rocking back and forth, wailing. In his arms was the limp body of Moshe ibn Daud.

"No one may speak to my father," Mayah told all visitors the next day. "It would do no good. He is inconsolable and the doctor has given him a sleeping draught to ease his grief."

Thus it fell to Mayah to deal with the friends who came to share their sorrow and the leaders of the Jewish community who came to investigate Moshe's death.

"I have no brothers or uncles in Córdoba to stand with me," she told Solomon when there was a break in the stream of people. "Can you stay until my father is better?"

He agreed. "But Mayah," he said, "I have questions, too. How did Moshe die? And what was he doing here so late?"

"The doctor says Moshe was stabbed once, directly through the heart," Mayah answered. "At least he could not have suffered greatly."

Solomon pitied her but pressed on.

"And my second question?"

Mayah rubbed her tired eyes. She would not allow the respite of healing sleep. "Why was he here? Father told me he had sent Moshe a letter,

begging him to come visit at the earliest opportunity. For some reason
he thinks Moshe couldn't wait until morning but flew to him at once."

"Apparently over the wall in the garden," Solomon commented.

"Yes," Mayah answered. "He must have. The guards at the gates
swear they never saw him. I believe them. Córdoba isn't a dangerous city.
The guards walk the perimeter of the garden only at the change of the
watch. Anyone could have climbed the wall."

"And that's what you're planning to tell the elders when they come
to find the murderer?"

"Mayah stared at him. "The what?"

"Mayah, you're far more affected by this than you think," Solomon
said in exasperation. "The man was stabbed though the heart. Do you
think he did it to himself?"

"I . . . I . . . don't . . . I didn't," Mayah's eyes were unfocused. She shook
her head to clear it. "I can only feel that Moshe is dead. Father was weeping over him. An accident or . . ."

"Or murder," Solomon finished cruelly. "The *tovim* will ask your father
why he sent for a young man in the middle of the night and why Moshe
didn't come to the gate. Any answer he gives will be unsatisfactory."

"He loved Moshe!" Mayah insisted.

"But Moshe didn't love him, did he, Mayah?" Solomon's tone was
softer now, filled with sympathy.

The look Mayah gave him was startling. He hadn't expected
defiance.

"Moshe loved the truth, Solomon," she answered fiercely. "Everything else came after that. His studies were all that mattered."

"More than you?" he asked.

Mayah gave him a bitter smile. "I love the truth, as well. That is what
we shared, not the vulgar union of the flesh that you're so fond of."

Solomon ignored the censure. "I don't understand," he admitted.
"But I still believe that the elders will assume that your father killed
Moshe because Moshe rejected him."

"Do you really believe my father is a murderer?"

The morning was gentle. The smell of orange blossoms from the tree
outside the window was pungent. The colors of the walls and curtains
were pastel, shades of dreams and spring. In Paris the winter was still
hard. Solomon wished he were back home. Instead he had to answer this
girl who loved truth.

"Unless the guards are lying," he said. "There was no one here but your slaves, in their own rooms at the back, and you and your father, whose rooms overlook the garden. And me," he added. "Therefore one of us must have killed him. I didn't."

Mayah stared at him in silence. Slowly she nodded.

"I see. But why should it be one of us? Why not another intruder? If Moshe climbed the wall, why not someone else?"

"Who?"

She shook her head in anger. "I don't know. A thief. A neighbor who thought Moshe was a thief. Solomon! I thought you were staying here to protect me from people who would ask questions like that!"

"There will be worse ones soon," Solomon told her. "If no one else can be found, your father will be charged in Moshe's death."

The *tovim*, leaders of the Jewish community, were kinder with Mayah that Solomon had been. They only asked a few questions about what she herself had heard and seen. They then promised to return the next day to interrogate Yishmael. Their expressions indicated that they wouldn't be as forbearing with him.

Solomon didn't want to believe that his old friend had murdered Moshe. Yishmael wasn't a man prone to quick anger. He wasn't one who would react with bitter jealousy if rejected. But what if he had taken Solomon's hint about Mayah and Moshe seriously? Would he have killed this boy he loved to protect his daughter?

Of course he would. Mayah was everything to him. *But did he?*

The other answer was that Mayah had done it, but Solomon found that impossible to imagine. What reason would she have to kill someone who loved her? Solomon remembered the way she had reacted to his touch the first night of his visit. Had Moshe attacked her? That seemed unlikely. But both Mayah and Moshe had been afraid of someone. If not her father, then who? Who might have followed the boy over the wall?

What if there was a thief, looking to steal not Moshe's property, but Moshe himself? Solomon decided to find out.

He went to the inn where the Norman was staying.

"Ranulf? Yes, he's here," the innkeeper told him. "In the back room with Ali ibn Tibbon."

Both men looked up in mild surprise as Solomon entered. Then the Norman's face lit up. He began to speak in rapid French.

"Ah, yes, the merchant from Paris!" he exclaimed. "You've decided to trade with me, after all. Wonderful!"

"No," Solomon answered. "I came to find out if you happened to return to the home of Yishmael ibn Samuel last night."

"No, of course not." The man appeared puzzled. "I was only there the once, when I met you. Why?"

"You showed a great deal of interest in the young man, Moshe ibn Yosef," Solomon said.

"Who didn't?" Ranulf asked.

"You wanted to buy him."

Ranulf nodded. "I thought of it. He's a bit old, but his talents combined with his physical attractiveness would make him very marketable. I might get as much as five hundred *bezants*." He looked hopefully at Solomon. "Do you know of a way it can be arranged?"

He must be either a superb liar or totally innocent. Regretfully, Solomon decided it was the latter. He told the men of Moshe's death.

"Ah, so that's why you wanted to know where I was last night," Ranulf said. "It would be easy to blame the infidel foreigner. Well, you can't. I was at a dinner with Ali until nearly dawn. There are many who will swear to it."

Ali nodded his confirmation. Solomon apologized for the intrusion and left.

He went back to the house, where he found Yishmael still sleeping and Mayah sitting alone in her room. On a table next to her bed was a pile of parchment. She looked up sadly as Solomon entered.

"Moshe's notes, and mine," she told him. "We were working together on these most of the time, whatever your midden-sodden mind thought. Now I don't know what to do with them. Despite Master Gabriol's opinion, I believe in what Moshe was doing. I'd like to keep them, continue the study."

"Why don't you?"

Mayah rubbed her temples. "Right now, it hurts too much. I can't even bear to look at them. It might be better to give all these to Master Gabriol. He must consider himself of an age for philosophy and, of course, as Moshe's teacher, he is the one most likely to understand them. Moshe's work shouldn't be lost."

She looked at him and Solomon could tell she had been crying. Her grief was so much more honest and intense than Yishmael's. For a moment Solomon felt a flash of anger at the selfishness of his old friend, not to see his daughter's pain. Then he remembered that Mayah didn't want him to.

"Will you take these to the Master now?" she asked. "Before I change my mind. Anyway, if they come for my father, the house will be searched. I don't want to explain why Moshe's work is here."

It wasn't far to the home of Gabriol ibn Daud. Solomon walked slowly. It didn't seem right to turn over the results of the study Moshe and Mayah had made. He feared that Gabriol would take credit for the work his student had done. But then, as Mayah had said, what mattered was the truth.

He knocked at the gate, but no one answered. As he turned to go, Solomon heard someone shouting inside and smelled smoke.

"Fire!" he shouted. "Call out the neighborhood!"

Then, leaving the bundle of parchment by the gate, he lifted himself over the wall. At the top, he stopped and stared down at Master Gabriol.

The scholar was busy stuffing something into the bake oven behind the house. Standing next to him was a slave with a handful of thin sticks, pointed at one end.

"I tell you there were eight of them!" Gabriol yelled at the man. "What have you done with the last one? If you don't find it I will beat you senseless and sell you as a field worker in Egypt."

"I swear, Master," the man pleaded. "There were only seven in the box."

Gabriol hit him and the sticks scattered. Solomon dropped down from the wall and raced to pick them up. He had realized what they were.

"What are you doing here? Give me those!" Gabriol screeched. "Guard, guard!"

"They'll be here soon," Solomon said. "Along with the rest of the street. I've called out the firewatchers."

"You're insane!" Gabriol grabbed for the sticks. "I'll have you thrown in prison for breaking in here."

Solomon ignored the threats. He put the sticks into his left sleeve and knotted it. The slave had managed to get away, either to a safe hiding place or to rouse Gabriol's guards. There wasn't much time. Solomon pushed the teacher aside and began pulling pages from the oven.

"The parchment is lost, but the pages written on vellum haven't caught yet. It wasn't enough to kill him, you had to destroy his work as well?"

Gabriol leaped at him, but Solomon caught him easily and held him, arms pinioned, bent over the smoke.

"I have the eighth stick," he told the struggling man. "Moshe was setting them in Yishmael's garden to chart the pattern hidden in the stars. You caught him at it and were angry that he had disobeyed you. There was no moon that night and you missed one of the markers. Or was it the eighth stick that you drove into the poor boy's heart?"

"Insane!" Gabriol shrieked again, coughing in the smoke. He writhed in Solomon's grasp and managed to get an arm free. Instead of fighting back, the teacher used his free hand to push the remaining pages farther into the fire. Solomon pulled him back in horror.

"It's you who are mad!" he shouted. He picked up one of the pages he had saved. Greek, with some notes in Hebrew letters but words he couldn't read. Aramaic, perhaps.

"What do these say? What had Moshe found?"

"Nothing." Gabriol sank to the ground, weeping. "He was wrong, too young to attempt such study. It was all heresy, blasphemy, totally inaccurate. But Moshe, he believed it and he could make others believe it too. It had already corrupted him enough that he continued in his wayward actions even though I forbade them expressly. He had to be silenced. The Almighty never spoke to Pythagoras, or to the Arab Brethren. Only to us! You must understand, Solomon. How can we continue to survive in exile if we doubt that?"

Solomon shook his head. The guards had arrived, led by Gabriol's slave. Solomon raised his hands in surrender, but they didn't try to take him.

"We've sent for the elders," the slave told him.

"Good. Tell them I can be found at the home of Yishmael ibn Samuel."

Gabriol gave him a look of pure hatred.

"The elders will understand that it was necessary to stop Moshe before he went too far," he said firmly. "Belief in the unity of all philosophy would destroy us! I didn't kill Moshe: I saved him."

Mayah was waiting. Solomon gave her back the notes and told her what had happened. She listened without moving.

"My poor Moshe," she whispered. "At least he died for the truth."

"Did he?" Solomon asked. "How do we know? Perhaps Gabriol was right. Moshe may have misinterpreted what he read."

"Solomon!"

"But now that Moshe is dead and his theories with him," Solomon continued. "We'll never know, will we?"

Mayah smiled a sad smile and looked down at the pages in her hands. Solomon had brought back some of the vellum singed in the fire, as well.

"I will know," she said. "If I must spend the rest of my life searching."

"And if you find that Moshe was wrong?"

Mayah looked him directly in the eyes. "Then that will be the truth and I'll know I've honored his memory."

Solomon had no doubt that she would. A few days later, he left warm Córdoba for the icy North. As he went, he feared that, although he had found the solution to the murder, he had just been propelled into a greater mystery that he might never solve.

The road suddenly seemed much colder.

What's a Mystery Without Recipes?

I'm sometimes asked to add recipes to my stories. This isn't easy because most of the ones written at the time Catherine lived are medicinal and not something you'd want for dinner. However, I came up with a couple. This first one went with "Death Before Compline".

FEAST DAY FISH STEW

Ingredients:

About a pound of fish, any kind, whatever swims into your net. Fillet it and cut it into chunks.

Fresh herbs, whatever you have: parsley, basil, tarragon, watercress etc., chopped and mixed, about a cup.

2 cups white wine.

Vegetables: carrots, turnips, celery, onions, cabbage (no potatoes or corn), 2 cups or so sliced.

Salt and pepper to taste. (remember, pepper isn't cheap!)

Round loaves of whole-grain bread, tops sliced off and a hole dug to make a dish.

Breadcrumbs from the scooped-out part.

Directions:

Bring wine to a simmer in a large pot; add vegetables and cook on low heat for 20 minutes or until tender, add herbs and cook another 10 minutes. And fish chunks and heat until fish is done to your taste. Thicken with bread crumbs, if necessary. Season with salt and pepper.

Ladle stew into bread. Cover with the upper crust to keep it warm during the long walk from the kitchen to the dining room. Large loaves can be shared by two people. Eat with a spoon. When done, you may tear the bread and eat that, too. This recipe should serve about four, although a hardworking person of the Middle Ages could eat the whole thing with no problem. They would also have simply cleaned the fish, maybe chopped off the head and tail, and thrown it in the pot. The head and tail could be used for broth or charity. You can give the leftover bread, soaked in the stew sauce, to the poor at your gate, as well.

Templar Roast Lamb

I can't imagine why I forgot to put recipes into my book *The Real History Behind the Templars*. People are curious about every other aspect of the lives of those knights. Their diet should also be of interest. Since my non-fiction history of them takes care of everything else, I'm grateful to Joan Hess for allowing me to make up this lack in her mystery writers cookbook.

The Templars were a group of knights who came to Jerusalem after the First Crusade and stayed to protect pilgrims coming from Europe. They eventually became monks who answered to the pope and took vows of poverty, chastity, and obedience. They also remained fighting knights and took part in most of the battles of the Crusades. They came to a sad end, as the book explains. Today they are the subject of novels, movies, and innumerable theories involving lost treasure and secret societies.

I don't think any of those involve recipes, either. However, since the Templars were fighting men, they were allowed meat, unlike other monks, who just sat around, copied manuscripts and gossiped and, therefore, didn't need much protein. So here is a likely main course for the Templar knights in Jerusalem.

Ingredients:

1 leg of lamb, about six lbs.

1 lemon cut in half

1 tsp cinnamon

1 tsp ground ginger

1 tsp ground nutmeg

2 tsp ground cumin

1 tsp coarsely ground black pepper

2 tsp sea salt (kosher salt will do)

Red wine

Preheat oven to 500 degrees or start up a grill or build a fire and set up a spit, whatever suits your life style.

With a sharp knife cut deep slices in the lamb about ½ inch wide.

Rub the lemon half over the meat, squeezing the juice into the cuts.

Mix the spices in a dish and then rub the mixture all over the lamb, again seeing that some of it gets into the cuts.

Put it on a rack in the oven or on the grill or spit it for the open fire.

If you put it in the oven, cook it for ten minutes at 500 then turn the heat down to 350.

Baste with the wine every 20 minutes or so.

Cooking time will vary depending on how you cook it, whether you like your lamb bloody, pink, or well-done and if there is an army at the gates that you didn't invite for dinner.

Lavender-Scented Candles

While this isn't a recipe for food, I am adding it in case anyone wishes to get medieval in candle-making. Rich people had candles from beeswax, but even they didn't use them every day. Tallow candles were much more common.

There are a number of ways to make candles. First you need something to put a wick in. You can go to your local slaughterhouse and see about getting fresh tallow, sheep or beef for preference. Then you render it and toss out the crunchy bits.

If you want something finer and more expensive, you can get a bee-keeper to sell you some bee comb, after she's taken out the honey. This is also rendered and dead bees tossed out. Or sometimes the comb is just rolled tightly about a wick.

The wick is a piece of string that has been soaked in the wax or tallow.

These days you can also go to the store and buy paraffin, an oil byproduct.

OK, you have a wick and some liquid wax substance. Tie the wick to a rod (I use a chopstick) and balance it over the center of the mold. You can buy metal molds at a craft shop or use a can or old milk carton. Put a few drops of essence of lavender in the melted wax. You can also add some sprigs of fresh lavender. Pour the wax over the wick into the mold and let cool. Slip the candle from the mold, clip the top of the wick and light.

CPSIA information can be obtained at www.ICGtesting.com
Printed in the USA
LVOW040029300113

317802LV00004B/6/P